LOVE
like
THAT

LOVE

like

THAT

stories

EMMA

DUFFY-COMPARONE

HENRY HOLT AND COMPANY
NEW YORK

Henry Holt and Company
Publishers since 1866
120 Broadway
New York, New York 10271
www.henryholt.com

Henry Holt® and ® are registered trademarks of
Macmillan Publishing Group, LLC.

Library of Congress Cataloging-in-Publication Data

Names: Duffy-Comparone, Emma, 1988- author.
Title: Love like that : stories / Emma Duffy-Comparone.
Description: First edition. | New York : Henry Holt and Company, 2021.
Identifiers: LCCN 2020009968 (print) | LCCN 2020009969 (ebook) | ISBN
   9781250624550 (hardcover) | ISBN 9781250624543 (ebook)
Classification: LCC PS3604.U383 A6 2021 (print) | LCC PS3604.U383 (ebook) |
   DDC 813/.6—dc23
LC record available at https://lccn.loc.gov/2020009968
LC ebook record available at https://lccn.loc.gov/2020009969

Our books may be purchased in bulk for promotional, educational, or
business use. Please contact your local bookseller or the Macmillan Cor-
porate and Premium Sales Department at (800) 221-7945, extension 5442,
or by email at MacmillanSpecialMarkets@macmillan.com.

These stories have been previously published in slightly
different form in the following publications:
"The Zen Thing": *One Story* and *The Pushcart Prize XXXIX*; "Marvel Sands": *The
Sun*; "Sure, Fine": *American Scholar*; "The Package Deal": *New England Review*;
"The Offering" (originally "The Sacrifice"): *AGNI*; "Exuma": *Mississippi Review*;
"Love Like That" (originally "The Blue Bowl"): *Ploughshares*; "Plagiarism": *The
Sun*; "The Devil's Triangle": *New England Review* and *The Pushcart Prize XLI*

First Edition 2021

Designed by Omar Chapa

Printed in the United States of America

1   3   5   7   9   10   8   6   4   2

for my parents and for my sister
and for Dave

CONTENTS

LOVE

like

THAT

THE ZEN THING

Each year, the family unpacks itself for a weekend on a beach and pretends to have a good time. This summer they are in Rhode Island, on Scarborough Beach. Everyone is staying at the Sea Breeze Motel down the street. Expectations are low. It is the kind of setup where doors open onto a courtyard, which is carpeted. In the middle of the carpet is a pool. In the middle of the pool, submerged, are a bikini bottom and a swimming noodle, which has somehow drowned like a piece of plumbing pipe.

Penny, Anita's sister, who is thirteen and has Down syndrome, has spent the morning dipping a red bucket into the pool and watering all of the plastic plants with it: the schefleras in the corner, and a few palms slouching under the exit signs. She wears an industrial measuring tape clipped to her bathing suit and has measured the diving board several times and the circumference of the doorknobs to their rooms. Anita adores Penny.

"She's really concerned about maintenance these days." Anita's mother sighs. "And penises."

Anita and her boyfriend, Luke, have driven down from Maine for the day. Five months ago, after their two-year affair, Luke left his wife for Anita, and they fled to a friend's empty cabin in Harpswell, where they have been staying ever since. Luke is twenty-five years older than Anita and was her art professor. As it is with this kind of thing, Anita is finding the narrative of an affair much more reasonable than the living of it, which is, when you get right down to it, a clusterfuck. She is twenty-three. Her period is late. It is an unfortunate and terrifying thing, much like the six-pack Luke has taken to drinking each morning before he calls his daughter, Matilda, who is eight, and who, because he cannot bear to tell her, and because his wife is certain he will come back, still thinks he is on a business trip.

Everyone is supposed to meet in the courtyard and head down to the beach, which is across the street and over the rock wall. There are a dozen plastic lawn chairs by the pool that have yellowed like teeth. Anita's grandmother is sitting in one of them. She is dressed all in white—pants and sweater and shoes—and is breathing heavily. She is staring at Luke. Since his haircut, which makes him look like an Irish cop, he seems to be grayer than ever, especially around his temples.

"You look like that actor," Anita's grandmother says to him. She has already said it twice.

"Oh, I doubt it," Luke says, but she nods. She has already complimented his eyes and his chin. She doesn't know he is married, or really anything about him at all. Her husband, Frank, is there, too. When Frank speaks, he leaves little white spots on the shirt of whomever he is talking to, and he says, "I was going to say the exact same thing," after anyone speaks. He and Anita's grandmother are eighty years old. They met five years ago, at Twin Rivers Casino. Her grandmother loves Frank, and everyone is glad for it, especially Frank, who seems to have no family to his name whatsoever and will now, he knows, have his ass wiped by Anita's parents when the time comes. He has already asked Anita's mother, who is a nurse, to be his medical power of attorney.

"You okay, Gram?" Anita asks. Her grandmother has been moaning and belching all morning.

"I've got, you know, the dysentery," she says. She is reattaching her Italian horn pin, which Anita has always thought looked like a little dick on a chain.

"It's just diarrhea, Ma," says Anita's mother. "Not the trenches. Stop eating all those goddamn fried scallops." Anita's mother is turning sixty next month and is not doing well with this. She has been talking a lot about her own father lately, who left the family when she was eleven and later died before she could get around to forgiving him. Once a week she has been going to Boston to see a psychic, which, Anita knows, has less to do with death and more to do with Anita. The offense, however, is unclear: the affair or simply moving out of the house. Now that her older daughters are gone, Anita's mother says, she has no one to talk to, and Penny, God love her, sometimes makes her want to get the gun. She also still gets hot flashes, which she calls HFs, and which make her stop whatever she is doing, unhitch her bra, and whip it out of her sleeve like a rabbit from a hat.

"She's a complex woman" is all Anita's father has to say about any of it. He is still having difficulty processing that his daughter is having sex with a man five years younger than he is. Anita knows this because her mother told her so. She can't blame him, really.

Theresa, Anita's sister, has been applying suntan lotion to her chest with one finger, careful not to smear any on her bathing suit. She is wearing sunglasses that are too big for her face, which seems to telegraph just how expensive they are. Theresa is thirty-one, and after a decade of casting about in pills and low self-esteem in Belize, she has suddenly pulled a life together for herself. She has moved back East with her new husband, Trey, who makes lots of money reselling life insurance policies. He has several life-size oil paintings of George Washington in their house.

"They change hues depending on the time of day," Trey explained earlier.

"That must really be something," Anita said.

Trey makes many dishes with truffles and drinks only German wine. He is considering pursuing a PhD in economics at Brown. Or Columbia or Harvard or Dartmouth. He also is a Libertarian, and though no one really understands what that means, they know it is scarier than a Republican. Theresa and Trey have one child, Francine, who is two and apparently has a lazy eye, though no one knows what Theresa is talking about. The corrective surgery is scheduled for next month at Mass. Eye and Ear.

They all make their way across the street and begin to climb over the rock wall because Anita's father does not want to pay the ten dollars to park for the day. Luke hands the beach bag to Anita and helps her grandmother navigate a boulder.

"Thank you, Luke," says Anita's mother. Anita can tell by the way she looks at Luke that her mother is mourning for Ben, Anita's boyfriend of seven years, who lived down the street and came over for dinner almost every night. Anita's mother has written Ben several letters and has told Anita that, though she knows it is inappropriate, she hopes sometime he can come over for dinner. She has no idea that Anita cheated on him for a year at the Best Western two blocks from the house. Neither does Ben, who emailed Anita last week to say that he is still in love with her. She has been thinking about this situation more than she would like to admit. She has been trying to remember what was so bad about him in the first place. True, he pronounced *supposedly* "supposably." He gave her noogies sometimes. Once, when she asked him if he found her attractive, he said, "I like the buttons on your jacket." Still, when she is fifty, he will be only fifty-two.

"Isn't he lovely?" her grandmother says of Luke, who is wrapping his arm around her hips and hoisting her over the wall. Anita nods. He is. Sometimes she cannot believe she is finally with him. Her friends are all excited for her. They consider it a fairy tale, and while Anita agrees that it is remarkable, they were not with her in Maine, in December, trying to start a fire with used Kleenex, while Luke sat on the kitchen floor and asked her over and over if children of divorced parents ended up in mental institutions. They have not been there when he goes for long jogs in the dark, so long that she sometimes drives around looking for him, like last night, when she found him on the side of the road, sitting on half of a blue buoy, sobbing into his hands.

Anita's father is already down on the beach, setting up umbrellas. His technique is to stick the pole in the sand and then hit it hard with a hammer. Penny loves to help with this. She has taken out her tape measure and is measuring the pole and their father's feet. Her father is the only one with truly olive skin, but when he sits down, his stomach folds in on itself, and so it has tanned in a marble effect. He is kind and quiet and loves her mother more than Anita can ever imagine being loved by anyone. The few times he has met Luke, he has been cordial. Last month, Anita's parents invited Luke and Anita over for dinner, where everyone talked about the Gulf War except Anita, who smiled and knew little about the Gulf War because, Jesus Christ, she was two.

The family is setting up its own stations, laying down blankets and unfolding beach chairs. Anita's mother grabs the hammer from Penny, who has been offering to check people's reflexes with it, and throws it into the rocks. Luke is still lagging behind with Anita's grandmother and waving his arms in the air the way he does when he is talking about something that excites him. He is the most earnest person Anita has ever met. He is gentle and curious and frequently undone by factual tidbits from the BBC. Luke quotes Rumi sometimes about how "love is a madman" and says anyone who doesn't get that can go fuck themselves. Sometimes, he just stares at Anita and sighs. She loves this, but when she considers his fifty thousand dollars' worth of credit card debt, or the beer bottle caps strewn across the floor of his car like scabs, or the picture of his wife and daughter that fell out of his wallet when he went to pay for gas this morning, Anita marvels at how quickly she has fucked up her life.

Anita walks toward Luke and her grandmother. Crabs pop in and out of holes, lugging their fiddles. Even crabs have baggage, she thinks. It isn't anything new. Anita's grandmother points to the afternoon moon, stuck in the sky like a plate. "Remember when you used to think there were fish on the moon?" she says. She pats Anita's arm.

"No."

"You thought the craters were lakes. You were always talking about all the fish on the moon, even though I told you there weren't any."

"Okay, Gram," Anita says.

The women are all helmeted in beach hats. Anita's grandmother eases herself into a chair that someone has set up for her. She is still wearing shoes and socks. Frank is already helping himself to one of the sandwiches Anita's mother has packed in a cooler. Frank has a colostomy bag, which Anita imagines strapped like an animal to his body. Though she knows not everyone will end up with one of these, for her it has come to represent, like a piece of postmodern art, everything that is horrible about aging. Anita watches Frank chew and then she imagines the remnants of the tomato-and-cheese sandwich sitting hot and runny under his shirt. When Luke is his age, Anita will be only fifty-five, which is something she has taken to weeping about in the bathroom after Luke has fallen asleep. She has never been good at the Zen thing. She has, since she can remember, anticipated the deterioration and death of everyone she loves. Now, she realizes, her parents and her husband (if he ever gets divorced) will all be in a nursing home at the same time. Maybe she will be able to get a group rate. Her own mother is fifty-nine and seems very, very young. She still gets her period sometimes, for Christ's sake. For a minute, Anita tries to imagine her mother married to Frank instead of her father, but it seems too fucked for words.

Anita's father and Trey are standing down where the sand is wet, talking about insurance options, and Luke has wandered over, carefully sidestepping a castle, his hands in his pockets. She watches him bow his head as he starts to listen, trying to get the gist of things, nodding occasionally. She knows that even if he has no idea what they are talking about, he will figure it out and say something intelligent. It is one of the reasons she loves him. He is wearing running shorts that they bought last night at Goodwill. They have a patch that says "England" on the front, which is probably covering some scary stain. He looks good in them, though, Anita notices. He looks good in everything.

Anita's mother sits down, her pubic hair extremely visible. Anita tries to catch Theresa's eye, to share a joke about it as they always have, but Theresa is busy with Francine, whose diaper is already packed with sand.

"What did I say about that?" she is saying. "What did I say?" She has turned into an important, scolding mother. Anita liked her sister better when she wore a Bud Light bikini and made great mixtapes, when they stayed up late watching movies and scratching each other's back for ten minutes apiece.

"It's the beach," Anita says to Theresa. "There's sand."

"Yeah, well," Theresa says, standing up and adjusting her bathing suit. "I'm trying to be a parent, here." She glares at Luke, but Anita pretends not to notice.

"Why don't you two play rummy?" Anita's mother says, and digs into her bag for a deck of cards. "I love having my girls around me."

Anita sits down on the blanket. Francine toddles off toward Trey, and Theresa sits down, too, picking grains of sand, one by one, off her arm. She is most likely afraid they will interfere with her tan. Her diamond is a sparkling mouse on her finger.

"So, are you painting these days?"

"Sort of," Anita says. Her canvases and brushes are in the trunk of her car. She has not touched them for five months. She has found herself too anxious to do anything except clean the kitchen. She is going to apply to grad school in the fall, no matter what happens. She has promised herself this much.

"How's the job?" Theresa asks. Theresa doesn't have to work anymore, though she has a way of making this seem a natural thing, as if everyone has forgotten that she worked at a gas station for eight years.

"It's temporary," Anita says. Until she and Luke figure out where to live, she has been bagging groceries at the Hannaford supermarket in Brunswick. She is not even a cashier yet. She makes eight dollars an hour. She works forty hours a week, because Luke is still sending all of his paycheck to his wife. He hasn't worked that part out yet. He hasn't worked any of the parts out yet.

"It's all *temporary*," Theresa says. "That much is clear."

"Who wants a soda?" Anita's mother asks.

"Not me," Theresa says. "I am trying to get to one hundred and forty pounds. As much as I try, I just *cannot* get there. It is maddening."

Anita has no idea who Theresa is anymore. She never used to say things like *maddening*. She used to say things like *fuck muppet*.

"I don't want to hear that," Anita's mother says. "You are a beautiful weight." She thinks her dark sunglasses hide the fact that she is staring at people, but it is obvious because her mouth hangs open a little when she does it. Anita knows she is watching Luke.

Penny runs over and lands on her knees, her cheeks creamy with sunscreen. She crawls over the blanket toward Anita and gives her a long hug.

"I love my Anita," she says.

"I love my Penny," Anita says, and squeezes her back.

"Don't grow a penis," Penny says gravely, holding Anita's face close. She is wearing braces.

"What?" says Anita. She looks at her mother.

"If you grow a penis like Sandy in that movie," Penny says, "you're going to kill yourself!" She begins to cry, her hands in fists by her knees. "And you won't be able to find a job!"

Anita's mother wags a Kleenex at Penny, who takes it and presses it over her eyes and mouth. The Kleenex moves up and down over her face like a heartbeat. "It's LGTBZ-whatever-the-fuck week at her school," Anita's mother says. "Trans awareness."

Theresa groans and looks down the beach. She has a strip of zinc on her nose, and her chest is pink. She looks so severe and matronly that Anita has to look away.

"We're all keeping our vaginas, Penny, we've been over this," Anita's mother says. "You, me, Anita, Theresa, Francine, and Gram."

"What's going on?" Anita's grandmother asks.

"Nothing, Ma," Anita's mother says. "Go back to sleep."

"What a sweet girl," Anita's grandmother says.

Frank is eating the second half of his sandwich. His hands are trembling. Penny makes him nervous. When she comes around, Frank's lips jump like crickets.

"So now what?" Theresa says. "She thinks she's queer?"

"Don't be like that," Anita's mother says.

"I don't think you can say *queer*," Anita says.

"What do you think the Q is?"

"I think it depends who says it," says Anita. "Like, when *you* say it—"

"Don't you monitor what goes on at that school at all?" Theresa says to their mother. "She's too sensitive. You have to stay on top of these things."

"Oh, really?" Anita's mother says. "Jesus Christ, I'm doing what I can! You try this." She throws her arms out and motions all around her. "You try dealing with all of this every goddamn day!"

"Fine."

"You're burning," Anita's mother says. She points to Theresa's chest. "There and there."

"So are you," Theresa says.

"I am not," Anita's mother says. "I'm having a fucking HF, all right?" She throws her beach hat onto the blanket and starts marching toward the water. Her hair is flattened to her head, as if in a net. Penny scrambles to her feet, the Kleenex fluttering to the sand, and follows.

"What's an HF?" Theresa asks.

"A hot flash," Anita says. "Give her a break."

"*You* give her a break." Theresa stands up, too, and points to Luke, who is telling a story to Anita's father and Trey. Everyone is laughing, and he seems encouraged by this. "Mom calls me every other day in tears," Theresa says. "You're killing her."

"You're a little too much, you know that?"

"What do you think you're doing with What's-his-name?"

"You know his name."

"Do you think you're in a novel, Anita?" Theresa says. "Look at your life." With that, she brushes off her ass and staggers across the sand toward her husband.

Luke is coming back now. He is pulling his shirt up over his head. "Your dad wants to go bodysurfing," he says. He looks exhausted but not unhappy, which is, Anita realizes, how he has looked for the past five months. But there is also a pain in his eyes that frightens her. He hands her his shirt, and she starts to press it to her face but stops. With Ben she could show affection, but with Luke she feels off-color and conspicuous.

"You okay?" he asks.

"Fine. You?"

He nods. "You're a poem," he says. "You going to swim?"

"Okay," she says, and takes off her dress. He stands back and makes a little shape of an hourglass with his hands. Then he walks to the cooler.

"Hey, Tim," he yells down to her father, who is standing by the water. "Want a beer first?"

Anita's father shakes his head and pushes his hand through the air. "No thanks!"

"It's eleven," Anita says.

"So what?"

"I know you do this at home, but don't do it here."

Luke shuts his eyes and pinches the bridge of his nose. He stays like that for a while. "Please," he says finally. "I don't need this right now." Then he starts down the beach. Trey and Anita's father are limping into the water, clapping their hands and hooting. The waves are bruised with seaweed. Penny is picking up tufts of it and throwing them. Theresa has waded only as far in as her ankles, holding Francine. She never gets in the water. She doesn't like to swim.

Anita's mother floats in the water, just a head and two feet, looking out to sea.

Anita stands in the sand. Her grandmother and Frank are both asleep under umbrellas. They have matching hairdos, and their skin is white and sunken, their mouths pulled in. Ben used to joke that if he looked quickly, he couldn't tell them apart. She finds a bottle of water in a bag and drinks from it. She is light-headed and can feel a zit on her chin, tender and zippy, like a spring bulb. She sits down in her mother's chair in the shade and looks across the beach, which is quickly filling in around her. She watches children crouch and slap their hands in the tide pool that is winding across the flats. All the women, breasts heavy and tired in their suits, pull wagons and strollers across the sand and begin to set up for the day. Everything is a production. There is sunscreen. There are so many toys.

Luke and Trey and Anita's father are bodysurfing. She watches the men stand and wait for the waves, then leap in front of them and swim hard until they're driven under the water. As a child it had alarmed her, watching her father wash ashore like a corpse. He is the best surfer, but Luke is good. He is a strong swimmer. She watches him crawl out of the froth and adjust his shorts. He has a way about him that is younger even than Trey. A few little girls run into the water near him, dragging boogie boards by their leashes, and Anita wants to shield Luke from them. But this is silly, she knows. He thinks about Matilda all the time.

Frank has woken up, and so has Anita's grandmother. They are flushed in their acrylic sweaters and press their lips together in a groggy way. They look lost and small.

"Oh, dear," Frank is saying. He is looking down at his waist. "Oh, no."

"What is it?" Anita's grandmother asks. She is peering over his chair and looking down. Anita decides, then and there, that if he has an erection she will kill herself. She will find a lot of rocks and put them in her pockets. Late period or not.

Her grandmother is standing up now. Frank is moving around in his chair.

"What's wrong?" Anita asks.

"Get your mother," Anita's grandmother says.

"What is it?" Anita has stood up.

"It's his bag," she says.

Anita jogs across the sand, darting between towels, and calls for her mother, who has walked out of the water and is now talking to Theresa and tugging at Francine's toes.

"Ma," Anita says. "It's Frank."

"What?"

Anita knows her mother isn't a fan of Frank. She thinks he is a phony and a taker. "Something about his bag," Anita says. "I didn't want to look."

She closes her eyes. "Frank's bag o' fucking tricks," she says.

Anita laughs.

"I'm all set with this day, I think," Anita's mother says, and starts trudging toward the chairs.

Anita's grandmother is in tears, flapping a Kleenex in the air. "Oh," she says. "Oh."

"Relax, Ma," Anita's mother says. Anita knows her mother hates this kind of thing, even though she is a nurse. "Let's see what's going on, Frank." Frank pulls up his shirt past his nipples. Anita's mother gets some napkins and a bottle of water. "Let's just clean it up a little, and then we'll get some soap from the bathroom." Anita stands aside. Her head is pounding, a woodpecker at her eyes. She doesn't know whom she pities most. She thinks about bodies, the failed mechanics of them. The second infancy. "It's fine," Anita's mother says. "The seal wasn't tight, that's all. Everything is fine. Ma, Jesus Christ, go sit down."

Theresa has come over now. "What's going on?" she asks.

"Frank's colostomy bag leaked or something," Anita says. "Mom's taking care of it."

"You want to deal yourself that hand?" Theresa whispers.

"Shut up, Theresa," Anita says.

Penny has pushed to the front of the action and is looking down at Frank. She has pulled out her measuring tape. "Thank you, Penny," Anita's mother says. "But I don't need your help." Penny doesn't move. She is staring. Then she begins to giggle. She laughs and claps her hands. She starts to fidget and then run in place, shrieking with delight. Anita's grandmother is moaning, covering her face with her hands.

"Oh, what a fucking scene," Anita's mother says. "Where's your father? Get him out of the water. I can't do everything here." Penny is now running around the blanket, whipping a handful of seaweed in the air. "Poopy belly button!" she cries. "Poopy Frank!" She stomps back to the blanket for another look. "Poopy—"

"Shut up!" Anita yells, and hits her across the face. There is the sound of wet skin. It is something between a slap and a punch. Her own hand stings. She thinks she might throw up. Everyone is quiet. Then Penny begins to sob.

"Classy, Anita," Theresa says. Anita's mother is still kneeling in front of Frank, dirty napkins in a fist. Her mouth looks blurry. She has licked off her lipstick, which she has worn every day since Penny was born.

Penny is hysterical now, holding her cheek and wailing. "I hate you," she cries, pointing at Anita. "I hate you!"

"You people," Theresa says. She bends over, grabs a towel, and folds it. Then she throws it back on the blanket. She goes to Penny and puts her arm around her shoulders. "I don't think Anita meant it, Penny."

Anita's father has arrived now, and Trey and Francine. "Get Francine out of here," Theresa says to Trey, rubbing Penny's back. He backs away, mouth open. People up and down the beach are turning now to look at Penny, who is shrieking.

"Penny, honey," Anita says. She goes to her, but Penny puts her hands up.

"I don't want you!" she cries. She is standing with her feet tight together. She points with both hands at Anita, like pistols. "I hope you die!" Penny points to Frank and Anita's grandmother, then Anita's mother and father, then Trey and Francine and Theresa. "I hope you die and you die and you!"

Anita can hear radio static, and somewhere the dull clatter of plastic pails. She watches the silver waves fold over each other, a man sprint a kite into the air, and behind him, Luke, who is walking toward the family. Water is dripping from his arms, and as he reaches Anita's side he is breathing hard from the cold. When Penny points her fingers at him and makes a lippy, popping sound of a gun, Luke grips his heart and falls to his knees, gasping. Anita watches him as he crumples sideways onto the sand, playfully twitching his feet until they lie still. Penny stops crying and stares. So does everyone else, including Frank, who is clutching a floppy sunhat to his waist.

Then Anita laughs.

MARVEL SANDS

After my dad ran off with a bank teller with great teeth, my mom and I moved in with this guy, Ronny. I was fifteen and needed money, so I took a job at Marvel Sands State Beach. During the day I sat in a booth at the entrance of the parking lot and sold tickets. I liked it out there, especially in the morning when sea smoke curled around the booth.

I picked up trash in the parking lot before the cars came. I strolled along the hedges that divided the lot from the marsh, pinching cigarette butts and straws and plastic cups with long metal pickers and dropping them in the black trash bag I dragged behind me. I always stopped to smell the beach roses. Once in a while a bee would be sitting in the yellow center like a pearl.

Seagulls always gathered in the parking lot. Some shuffled around; others jumped and then landed a few feet away. They had hard, watery eyes and beaks bowed like frowns. Some pecked at soggy hot dog rolls or peered inside slushie cups.

I whistled a lot when I was alone. I had a whole repertoire of songs, jazz standards like "Someone to Watch Over Me" and "Love Walked In." They made me happy, and I imagined I was in love. I whistled so I didn't have to think about other things, like my mother sitting in the house staring at the television or playing solitaire on a tray. I think the seagulls liked the songs. Sometimes I just talked out loud about nothing in particular, imagining that they were listening and nodding away, as if they couldn't have said it better themselves. I hadn't had company like that in a while. Even if they were just birds, it was a welcome change.

I started out working weekends. Until school let out, I was the only employee. Around five o'clock on my first day, I watched the manager of the park leave the bathhouse, where his office was. Mr. Manuel was well over six feet tall, and he pounded his heels into the ground when he walked. He stopped and faced the building, studying the garden in front of the bathhouse with his hands on his lower back like a pregnant woman. He bent over and plucked dead leaves and pulled a few hollow stalks from each plant. When he was done, he scooped the twiggy pile into his arms and chucked it into the dumpster. The wind blew most of it back into his face, and I heard him yell out, "Asshole!" Then he climbed into his massive red F-350 and accelerated into the flock of seagulls, exploding them into the sky.

The booth was cylindrical, like a lighthouse, with blue shaker shingles and wavy glass windows. Mr. Manuel slammed his brakes in front of it so hard the truck carriage bucked on its wheels. His head was shaved, so his scalp ran into his thick neck. He was probably pushing sixty, but without any hair it was hard to tell. His left eyelid had a pink dot that seemed to push against his eyeball in a painful way.

"Dirty fuckers," he muttered, glaring up at a seagull that had perched on the roof. "They'll eat anything. I've seen them go to town on a diaper." He stared through the windshield and tapped his thumbs on the steering wheel. He seemed to be thinking deeply or else not at all. "Have you had any handicapped folks roll through yet?"

I said that I hadn't.

"Good," he said. "So look, they technically get in for free if they're state residents, but any fat bastard can get one of those decals. So when they drive up, just play dumb and ask for the ten dollars."

I watched him pick bits of the garden from his green state-issued shirt and flick them out the window. One of the front pockets had an iron-on state park patch that looked like a kid's police badge. I felt a flutter of laughter in my chest and swallowed it.

"And tell them they have to park in a normal spot," he said. "Unless they really don't have legs or something. Obviously, show those poor fucks where the handicapped spots are. Wheelchairs aren't any picnic in the sand but that's their problem. And don't argue with folks about whether they have working legs or not. I already made that mistake." He scratched his chin. "I mean, how was I supposed to know some cars have pedals for your hands?"

I didn't know what to say. I watched a seagull peck under its wing. Two feathers sprang loose and floated to the pavement. He was the fattest one of the bunch. I decided to name him Gus, like the mouse in *Cinderella*.

"At six, count the money and write it down and put it in the safe. You have the key?" I nodded, reaching into the pocket of my khaki shorts for the lanyard.

"Make sure you count it right. Last year some clown couldn't do math and I took it in the ass from Parks and Rec."

I slapped a mosquito on my forearm and wiped it on a shaker shingle.

"But you're probably good with numbers," he said, beginning to roll up his window. "You tall girls are always smart."

At six that night, I hosed down the showers, changing rooms, and foyer, steering the sand into the square traps in the middle of the floor and out the doors. The work was surprisingly physical. At one point I looked at myself in a mirror. My neck and throat were red. My hair was frizzed. I bent over and soaked my head with the hose. Within minutes my scalp felt hot again.

In the bathrooms I dragged the webbed floor mats out of each stall. The mats were wide and heavy and left black marks on my arms. I poked the nuggets of wet toilet paper loose and hung each mat on its designated hook. Then I emptied the "birdhouses," stuffed with sanitary pads, diapers, and the occasional abandoned underwear, and I sprayed the insides with Lysol. I wiped down the toilets and sprinkled Comet into the bowls and swished it around with a brush.

Then I swept and mopped Mr. Manuel's office, with its framed photographs of the beach during hurricanes: a lifeguard chair strewn on the jetty, waves suspended mid-crash over the rocks like white claws, purple tufts of seaweed dangling from the shutters of the bathhouse. The back wall was covered with photographs of lifeguards from past summers. They were always posing on the jetty with a man with long black hair who was usually touching a bare leg or two. The women looked glamorous, with big breasts and little strips of tooth-white skin along their hip bones and cleavage. After studying the pictures, I realized the man was Mr. Manuel.

I emptied Mr. Manuel's trash and closed his office door. RELAX, someone had painted on the door with stencils, YOUR AT THE BEACH! JUST HAVE A GOOD DAY. The missing apostrophe and *e* were squeezed in with a Sharpie.

I biked the coastal route home, past stone mansions with pillars and ChemLawns and small cottages in the back for servants. The road curved, and in some spots the shoulders dropped straight down onto the rocks. The air was sharp with salt, and I inhaled deeply, feeling okay about things, unzipping my sweatshirt to let the breeze reach my neck as I pedaled.

The next morning, as I leaned my bike against the fence and unclasped my helmet, I saw Mr. Manuel watching me through his streaked window. I didn't wave, and neither did he.

The bathhouse had high ceilings with wide skylights. Fans whirred in circles and made quick shadows on the blue cement floor. Red park benches were nailed down on each side of the foyer. On the walls, maps of the coastline were secured behind Plexiglas, with a big yellow arrow indicating our location. THE SPIGOT IS NOT A TEAT was stenciled in orange paint on the wall over the water fountain.

Mr. Manuel was in his office, hunched over his desk, working on a crossword puzzle and clutching a bottle of Pepsi One. He looked up at me and swiveled slowly in his chair. He was wearing mirrored sunglasses with leather straps like pilot's goggles. I couldn't tell if I was supposed to laugh or not, so I didn't.

"I want to show you something, Ms. McMaster," he said. I followed him into the foyer. Green tribal tattoos circled both his calves. He led me to the third stall in the women's bathroom and pointed to a faint swirl of yellow sand on the floor.

"Do you see this?"

"I think so."

"This is unacceptable. Park visitors don't want to see a dirty floor."

"Right," I said. "I'm sorry. It won't happen again."

"Your second day, and you're already off to a shit start." He left me in the stall, and I stared at the sand. He returned with a broom and dustpan. "Sweep it up," he said, and he thrust them at me.

He was basically standing in the stall with me. There was barely any room to bend over. He just stood there with his arms crossed, staring at me through those ridiculous sunglasses. It was getting hot in that stall, so I bent over. My backside brushed against his leg but he didn't move out of the way. I could smell bleach and urine. The floor behind the toilet still hadn't dried from the night before. When I stood up, my forehead and cheeks itched.

"Good, good," he said, and backed out of the stall. I watched his tattooed calf muscles flex as he left.

I dumped the sand into the trash barrel, returned the broom and dustpan to the supply cabinet, and leaned on one of the shelves to steady myself. I looked out the open door and watched my helmet swing from the handlebars. If I quit, there was no guarantee I'd find another job, especially one where I would be left alone for the most part, and then I'd have to spend the weekends in Ronny's house.

Mr. Manuel's office door was closed. On the hallway floor sat the money tray and roll of tickets. I spent the rest of the day out in the booth, reading and feeding Gus and his friends stale bread I had brought from home. When Mr. Manuel drove through the gate at five, he didn't slow down to say good night.

When I got home, I could see the television flashing blue in the living room. Ronny rented one side of a defeated-looking duplex. A shutter was loose. A few hollowed evergreens climbed toward the second floor. The yard was as brown as the house.

My mother was knitting a sweater in the kitchen with the radio on low. She wore a thin nightgown with bunnies on it, and her hair was pulled back in a braid. A week before, she had slipped at the diner where she worked and cracked her tailbone. She was perched on an inflatable doughnut cushion so it could heal.

She smiled up at me and rested her needles on her lap. Blue wool strangled her pointer finger.

"How are you feeling?" I said. She craned her neck like a little bird to accept my kiss on her cheek.

"Real good," she said. "I even went for a walk today." She looked sick and haggard. Suspended on that doughnut, she looked like someone in a nursing home. I quickly smiled at her and turned away.

"How are the people?" she said.

"Fine. It's just my boss," I said, sitting down at the table to take my shoes off.

"Is she nice?"

"Yeah," I said. "She's all right."

"Are you hungry?" she said. "Ronny didn't want to wait, but I can fix you a sandwich."

"I think I'll go to bed," I said. My mom studied my face, but I pretended not to notice. I picked up my shoes and walked out of the kitchen.

Ronny was watching *SportsCenter* with his hairy legs on the coffee table and a bowl of cheese puffs on his lap. He was short with thick limbs and pockmarks on his face and a mustache that grew too far over his lips. He wore netted sports jerseys and hostile cologne. Next to his feet sat a sweating gin and tonic. He never used a coaster. His hand was resting in the bowl, pushing the puffs around like squeaking Styrofoam. I watched him wipe his fingers on a blanket my mom had knit.

I ran past him and up the stairs to my room. I opened all the windows and lay down on my bed and fell asleep with my clothes on. I woke at dawn to the garbage truck and thought of the way Mr. Manuel's green tattoos wrapped around his calves.

That May was warm. On my third weekend at Marvel Sands it reached eighty degrees. The booth was stifling, so I sat outside on the curb and greeted the cars and sold tickets. The parking lot filled up quickly, and I was able to read only two or three sentences at a time before being interrupted.

By three o'clock the air had shifted. Cold smoke ripped off the water. Gulls chased each other in threes and landed on the roof of the bathhouse. I was standing outside the booth, watching storm clouds gather in the west, and didn't hear Mr. Manuel coming to count the money. He grabbed a wad of twenties from the tray without a word and took it into the booth.

"The bills aren't facing the same way."

"I'm sorry, what?" I stepped into the doorway of the booth and looked at his shoulder blades.

"Get some Q-tips for those ears, Ms. McMaster. The bills, some of them are facing the wrong way. Fuck, some are even upside down." He shook his head and kept counting, flipping them over and turning them around as he went.

"I thought it was more important to get people through the line than arrange the money."

"You can't do both at the same time."

"No, I didn't mean—I can do both."

"Well, sharpen up. You don't seem to be trying very hard."

"Sorry," I said.

He turned around and took off his sunglasses. The sty was gone from his eyelid. His eyes were soft and surprised me.

"Come over here."

I stepped into the booth. It was just big enough for two people to fit inside. I stood there like an idiot.

"Come here, I said. It's all right."

I did. We were almost touching. His forearms were hairy and brown and muscular. He licked his thumb and reached for my face, and I flinched. He began rubbing just under my lower lip. He lifted my chin with the side of his finger and continued rubbing with his thumb. My eyes were in line with his, but I didn't look at him. I looked past his ear instead, out the window and all the way to the sea.

"Ink," he said.

The wet spot below my lip cooled as it dried.

Leaving for the night, Mr. Manuel stopped and leaned out his truck window. "It's a clusterfuck in the ladies' room," he said. He turned up some country song on the radio. "You chicks are animals," he said, and then puckered his lips like he was about to spit. "Expect to stay late tonight." He shifted into drive. "Make me proud," he added. I opened my book to a random page and gazed at the margins.

"You have a good face," he said. I clutched my book and stared dumbly. "I forgot your first name."

"Annie." It was just plain Ann, but I'd always wanted to be called Annie.

"You can call me Russ," he said, and I nodded.

At the exit he braked and idled for a moment, then drove away.

Hosing down the bathhouse was almost pleasant. The changing rooms with the showers didn't have roofs, and the white canvas curtains in the stalls buckled like sails. Above me, the clouds turned a muted pink.

It was a hot night, and I was sweating. I took off my shirt and shorts and turned on the water in one of the showers. I kept my bra and underwear on. I didn't like to be naked in a public place. I held my hair and let the water pummel the back of my neck. Wet, my underwear was transparent, and I felt more naked than I would have with nothing on at all. Paint chips dislodged from the bricks and spun wildly around the drain.

I put my clothes back on without drying off and finished cleaning. A seagull walked into the foyer and waddled around. It looked a lot bigger in the closed space than it would have outside. I clucked softly.

"Hey, honey," I whispered. "What are you doing in here?" It was eerie being alone with the bird in that room. I thought maybe it was a girl, not that I knew the difference.

I fished my half-eaten sandwich from the trash and tossed pieces onto the floor. The bird pecked at them and then wandered out the open door. I laughed out loud, locking the door behind me, and then biked home with no hands, the peepers pulsing at me from the marsh.

. . .

Ronny was in the front yard crazily sawing a two-by-four. He didn't look up at me as I walked into the house, and when I got to my room, my mom was sitting on my bed with her arm in a cast. All she told me was that her hand got slammed in the car door.

We didn't say much. She read from some romance novel while I brushed my teeth. Then she popped an extra-strength Tylenol and rubbed Vicks VapoRub over her chest and under her nostrils with her good hand. When she was done, she handed me the jar, and I screwed the cover back on and put it on my nightstand. Then she told me she was going to sleep with me for a while.

She stuck in her mouth guard, propped her arm on a few pillows, and sighed. I turned off the light and got into bed with her. My windows didn't have curtains, and the room was a bleak orange from the streetlights. My mom kept sitting up in the dark to inspect her cast, like she was looking for cracks. She moaned and sucked air through her teeth. I didn't know what to do except ask her if she wanted another pillow.

I pulled the sheet over my face and lay close to the mattress's edge so I wouldn't jostle my mom's hand by mistake. I thought of when she used to read storybooks to me in bed. She always kept her finger tucked behind the next page. My dad would have been around then. He'd have been downstairs, just two legs sticking out from under the wings of an open newspaper.

My mother didn't fall asleep for a long time. I didn't either. I could hear Ronny watching car racing in the living room. Once,

I pulled the sheet down past my eyes and looked at my mom. She was staring up at the ceiling. Sometimes she took a sharp breath like she was about to say something, but she never did.

On Memorial Day cars came to Marvel Sands at a steady pace, mostly SUVs with lots of happy kids and blow-up toys. They idled in line, tinted windows shut tight and air conditioners blasting. I couldn't sit down or eat. I couldn't put up an umbrella because Mr. Manuel said umbrellas were for fags.

Around noon a yellow Hummer pulled up. It drove so close to me that I had to leap out of its way. The driver was a woman in her forties with heavy makeup and a mannish haircut that was supposed to be sexy. Cellulite dimpled her stomach like tapioca. She was on her cell phone.

I stood there and waited, taking shallow breaths of exhaust. Tendrils of my hair stuck to my cheeks and neck. My eyes ached from squinting against the sun. While the woman talked, she thrust a state employee badge at me through the open window. She wanted half off. Technically she was entitled to it.

I stood there and watched as she pulled down the sun visor and grinned at herself in the mirror, checking her teeth for food.

"You need to sign here," I said, poking at my clipboard with a sweaty finger. The line of cars wrapped into the street. Mr. Manuel pushed a wheelbarrow full of bright red mulch across the parking lot. A mother with sunscreen-covered hands chased a screaming child. A group of old women with skirted bathing suits and floppy hats shuffled to the beach. I dug the clipboard into my jutted hip. She didn't seem to know I was there.

"You need to sign this sheet, or you won't get your discount." I was shouting like a nutjob. The woman seemed to register my presence for the first time. She grabbed my pen and made an X.

"That will be five dollars!"

She shoved a bill at me through the window. My ears were hot. My throat felt like I was trying to swallow a rose bush.

"How about you hang up and look at me?" I said.

"What did you just say?" She covered the mouthpiece of the phone, her face pinched with surprise.

"I said get off the damn phone." I scanned the parking lot and saw Mr. Manuel spreading mulch on the far side.

"I'll call you back, John," she said, and snapped the phone shut. Then she looked at me. "You've got a lot of nerve," she said.

"Yeah?" I said. "Well, you're a cunt." It came out in a mechanical way, like I was reading from a recipe. I had heard that word only in movies. I knew it was to be used sparingly and that it was a fighting word. Her lips parted in horror. Suddenly I couldn't focus my eyes. White lace crawled from the corners of my sight, and I blinked it clear. I didn't know this woman. She could have just gotten a divorce. Maybe she had cancer.

The woman chuckled and shifted into drive. "You won't have this job tomorrow, honey," she said.

I figured she was right. I didn't know what to do after she

drove off. I considered hopping on my bike and leaving, but I didn't have the energy. I sat down and stared at the money tray. The bills weren't all facing the same way. I decided to wait for Mr. Manuel to fire me.

Mr. Manuel hadn't left yet when I closed up the booth. I brought in the small stop sign and the sandwich board that listed ticket prices. I did everything slowly and deliberately, and then walked to the bathhouse, passing a group of seagulls sitting with their eyes closed.

Mr. Manuel didn't look up from his crossword puzzle. I placed the tray on his desk and listened to the clicking of the ceiling fan. He jammed the cap on his pen and then threw it across the room. It hit his *Playboy* calendar and slid down the wall.

"I like a girl with balls," he said finally.

"What?"

"You really gave that woman a good bitch slap, didn't you?" He laughed.

"Did she talk to you?"

"Yeah, she came howling. I took care of her. Gave her a guest pass, said I'd fire you."

"Oh," I said.

He gave me a smile, a weird one, and then grabbed a stack of twenties and started counting. "Now go fix the soap dispenser in the ladies' room," he muttered. "Just tape that fucker shut. Use the duct tape. And close my door. I have a headache."

In the bathroom, I taped the soap dispenser and wiped up

the greasy puddle on the floor. Then I walked outside and sat on the rock seawall and watched a tanker the size of a matchbox inch along the horizon.

I heard Mr. Manuel start his truck and leave for the night. I picked up my flip-flops and walked back to the bathhouse. I waited by the bathroom door for stragglers dragging beach bags and red children and then locked it from the inside.

After I finished hosing and cleaning the bathhouse, I decided to take a shower. I lifted my shirt over my head and dropped it on the floor. I stared at myself in the mirror. I had always wished my breasts were bigger, but standing there in my bra, I thought for the first time that they looked okay. Then I stepped out of my shorts and left my clothes in a heap.

While the shower was running, I unclasped my bra, wrung it out, and let it fall to the floor. I bent over and rolled my underwear down past my knees.

Then I heard the curtain rings slide along the rod.

Mr. Manuel was holding the curtain back, staring at me in the shower. His eyes traveled over my breasts and down my thighs. His face was expressionless. His lips were a thin line.

I didn't move. I didn't scream or cover my body with my hands. It was almost as if I had expected him to show up. I felt like I wasn't really in my body at all, yet I was very aware of it: I knew I hadn't shaved that high up my thighs. I knew the underwear looped around one ankle was part of the "days of the week" set. It might have been a Wednesday. I had never had to think about underwear before. I'd never had a boyfriend.

Mr. Manuel looked at me like he had every right to be there.

My arms hung at my sides. The water dripped from my nose and lips and nipples. We stood for what seemed like forever. I should have been mortified, but I wasn't.

I could smell his aftershave. I thought maybe I wanted him to touch me, but I wouldn't have known what to do. I thought maybe I wanted him to press me against the wall.

"I forgot my wallet," he said finally, staring at my mouth. "There's a seagull in the parking lot with a broken wing. When he dies, he'll start to stink up my park. After you're done here"—his eyes traveled down my thighs and back up to my face—"put the bird in a trash bag and hit it against the brick wall. One swing should do it."

Then he left.

I stood there with my eyes closed and the water pelting my skin.

I listened to the dull clap of waves against the jetty. The air was cool and smelled of fish. Storm clouds hovered over the showers. A few seagulls glided past, calling to me.

SURE, FINE

He took the good knives from Germany. He put his clothes in Tupperware containers fit for a moose. Into their original boxes went his wingtips. Ruth sat on the arm of the loveseat in her sweatpants, swinging her feet back and forth. She was not going to beg. She did not want to beg.

She begged a little.

"What gives you the right?" she said. "What gives you the fucking right?"

"You're all closed up," he said. "All your life you just sit in the backseat. I'm sick of driving."

"Okay," she said.

"Do you want to get married or not?" It had been eight years.

"Sure," she said. "Fine."

"*Sure?*" he said. "*Fine?*" He asked if he could have the loveseat.

"No," she said. But when she looked down, she barely recognized it. He had picked it. The Persian carpet, too, and the coffee table shaped like a whale. The treadmill and the food processor. The arborvitae out front, stoic as butlers. Ruth had never been one for decisions. She would wander through stores, holding up one bra and then another. "Which one do I like?" she would ask him, anyone, a teenage clerk hanging thongs like tinsel on a rack. "Which one do I want?"

"How about that one?" they would say. "You want that one." She would buy it, and then decide that maybe she didn't like it after all, and return it with the tags loose.

He gave her a long kiss: tongue and everything. She didn't think he'd actually leave. She called his bluff.

"Fine," she said. "Go."

He went. He put the knives in the backseat and the dog in front. He hitched the U-Haul to his bumper. Then she watched him and his bluff drive down the street.

She dragged a life she could barely claim to the edge of the street: a television, a headboard, a three-speed blender. She set up the kitchen table and two chairs on the sidewalk next to the recycling bins, sat down, and drank some Heinekens. CHEAP SHIT, her signs said. SOME CHEAP SHIT. Nearby, a squirrel palmed a nut like a basketball.

Not many people came. A woman stopped and got out of a Buick. She walked along the strip of lawn between the road and the sidewalk and ran her blue hands over everything. She had shaved her eyebrows and with a pencil had drawn a single line across her forehead in their place. Ruth noticed how important eyebrows were to a face. They either made it or they didn't.

The woman riffled through the boxes. She sniffed a paperback, broke wax off a candlestick, held up Ruth's vibrator and turned it on.

"Give me that," Ruth said. She stood up and knocked over her beer. She yanked the vibrator out of the woman's hand. "Where'd you get that?"

The woman bought two lamps and a pie dish.

"My husband's going to make me a lemon meringue," the woman said.

"Super," Ruth said.

When it got dark, Ruth sat on the curb. She could hear the mosquito patrol truck wailing up the hill, spraying the neighborhood, bullying the evening birds.

She went inside and shut the windows. She waited for the truck to pass. Chemicals roiled from the tank in a hemorrhage. After it was over, she went back outside and covered the remaining things with a tarp.

"Well," she said. "Good night."

In bed she grew dizzy, grief wide and sharp in her ribs, stuck there like a serving platter. Life could be full of such terrible things. You had to guard against them. You could, at fourteen, come home from work and find your father dead on the living room rug. You could stand there on an April day, a clutch of crocuses still dangling from your fist, and feel all that was light in you tighten to stone. You could watch your soul hobble out the back door.

The next day, she put all of her plants in the car (Molly and Maggie and Kevin: they were Irish, and dry) and moved back home to the Seacoast.

The attic had low ceilings and a milky skylight. To get up the stairs, she had to put her hands on the steps in front of her and crawl, crumbs of wallpaper catching on her sweater. She could hear a pigeon in the crawlspace, gurgling and knocking around. It freaked her out.

Her mother had tried to make the attic pretty. "At least call it the *third floor*, then." She'd put down a scatter rug and nailed two Klimt prints to the walls: *The Kiss* and one of some birches.

"Do you like it?" Ruth's mother asked. "I mean, not that you'd *like* it, but is it okay?"

"Yes," Ruth said. "Thank you." She gave her mother a hug. She squeezed her close, little bones. Later, Ruth put *The Kiss* in the closet.

The only bathroom was on the first floor. Ruth's mother had set up a commode in the corner under the window. "Is that what I think it is?" Ruth said.

"What, the commode?" Ruth's mother said.

"God help me," Ruth said.

"I found it outside the nursing home," Ruth's mother said. "I dragged it home on my walk!"

"No," Ruth said.

"It's perfectly clean."

"No." She was laughing now.

"You just sit in it like this." Ruth's mother squatted. She wobbled and clutched the windowsill.

"Fuck!" Ruth said.

She scheduled two interviews. The first was in an Alzheimer's facility. The woman interviewing Ruth kept her hands in fists and stared at them when she spoke.

"What are your aspirations?" she asked.

"My aspirations," Ruth said. She paused. "You mean, besides getting this job?"

"Your passions, desires?"

"Desires?" Ruth said. She thought about this. She couldn't think of anything, not even a lie. The woman stared at her and pushed her lips around. She pulled a box of Marlboros from her purse, pressed it to her nose, and then put it back.

"The beach," Ruth said finally. "I really like the beach." At the end, the woman told Ruth that they had already given the job to someone else. She just hadn't wanted to cancel last minute.

In her free hour, Ruth walked through town. She went into a Peruvian clothing store and started trying on hats. She tried on eight. She wasn't sure which one she liked. She thought maybe she wanted the red one with a felt rose on the brim. She looked like a flapper. Perhaps she had always wanted to be a flapper.

"Please don't try on the hats," said the man behind the desk, brushing his ponytail.

The Italian deli was gone. Her favorite card shop was

gone, too. Where there had been a hardware store there was now an artisanal cheese shop. In the square, by the water fountain, lots of mothers stood around with tight asses and ponytails. They looked younger than Ruth. They all wore black yoga pants. It was apparently trendy to be a stay-at-home mom in yoga pants. Feminism was a funny thing, Ruth thought.

She saw a woman she knew from high school pushing a stroller, and Ruth ducked inside the Bagelry until she passed. At the table, she pulled a hardboiled egg from her purse and shelled it. She covered it with pepper until it looked like a rock. Then she ate it, trying not to taste it too much.

The second interview was at the hospital, in the north wing. If she got the job, Ruth would have to sign a waiver agreeing to be quarantined if something serious broke out in the ward.

"Something serious like what?" Ruth asked. She could hear a stretcher whizzing down the hall: wheels schizophrenic in their casters, IV bags flapping.

"Who knows," the man said. He seemed to be trying very hard not to look at Ruth's breasts. When he did, he squeezed his little eyes and then opened them, wide, and beamed them at her forehead. "You could be contained for several months."

"Sure," she said. "Fine."

Ruth drove to the beach. She sat on the wall by the rocks and looked out at the Isles of Shoals. A condom and kite fin were burrowed in a head of seaweed. A whorl of sand fleas hung in the air, and she looked through it, out to sea, banging her heels into the cement. Her hair blew all around her face in the April wind. It caught in her mouth. It sliced her eyes until they watered.

She watched a couple by the shore. The man picked the woman up and ran into the water. Then he dumped her in the waves. She stood up, screaming, her hair blackened and flat on her shoulders. "*You bastard!*" Ruth heard her yell. The water was freezing, no doubt. The woman pulled her heavy, ballooning pants back up to her ass. Then she shoved him into the sand, and they kissed. They kissed like that for a while.

Ruth turned her head away. She glanced down the beach toward Nick's, the fish shack where she had worked in high school. She stood up, yanked her nylons into place, and walked across the parking lot and down the road.

Nick's looked exactly the same as it had nineteen years ago. On the roof, a large plaster tuna was still pulling a fisherman from his boat. The sign still said EAT oysters. The marsh, bitchy from the moon, had overflowed onto the parking lot. Water slinked around the dumpsters. A pile of cardboard boxes was soaked through, thick as cake.

Ruth walked up to the counter and ordered a side of fries. While she waited, she looked through the open wall into the kitchen. Two cooks stood on the line, a boy and a man. The boy pushed burgers around on the grill and slapped them flat with a spatula. The man shoveled fish into baskets and called numbers into a microphone. Ruth recognized his slouch. He whistled and drummed the counter with his fists. He turned up the radio and howled into his French fry scoop: *"Take me down to the paradise city, where the grass is green and the girls are pretty."* It was Eddy, of course it was.

Ruth found herself asking the girl at the counter for an application. She filled in her name and her phone number. *I worked here almost twenty years ago,* she scrawled on the bottom. As she handed it to the girl, Ruth watched Eddy drink from a glass of water. He spat out an ice cube. He spun the bill of his baseball hat to the back of his head, wet a dishtowel, and tucked it around his neck. He had to be, what—Ruth tried to calculate: he'd been twenty-seven when she was fourteen. That made him—*what*? She couldn't think. What did it matter now, really? It didn't. She looked at him again.

He hadn't changed at all.

She watched him slide along the floor and slam a handful of fish tails into the trash can. He looked up at Ruth. His eyes narrowed.

"You," he said.

Ruth waved, but she botched it and did a flap of sorts. She scowled at her shoes.

"She wants a job," said the girl at the cash register, her teeth black with metal. Braces made a wet, tragic thing of consonants, Ruth noticed. Braces made you sound drunk. She hadn't had them, herself. Her teeth were fine, mostly, except for the bottoms, which were crowded and sharp, like a bunch of house keys thrown together.

"Is that right?" Eddy said. He sidled back to the line, pulled a few slips from the wire, and studied them. He picked up his scoop, spun it in the air, and caught it. Then he slapped it against his apron. He waved Ruth in. She stepped through the kitchen door and right onto a breaded chicken patty. She felt damp and frantic, standing there in her skirt suit. She rubbed her neck. In the walk-in freezer years ago, he'd grabbed it and pressed his teeth into it. He'd clawed it with his fingers.

"Honestly," Ruth said. "I don't even live here."

"Where do you live, then?" he said. He threw a handful of oysters into some batter and tossed them.

"Chicago," she said. "Well, actually, a little closer recently."

"Julie," he said to the girl with the braces. "Get her an apron." She shrugged and trudged into the backroom.

"Christ, no," Ruth said. "I really—"

"You want a job or not, babe?"

The girl came back with an apron and offered it. Ruth took it, held it up, and examined it, as if it were a piece of scary lingerie.

"Put it on," he said. He took off his gloves and threw them onto the counter. Then he came up behind her and tied the strings. She could feel his fingers moving near her ass. Her hands trembled. "We're short today. Mercedes fucked up again."

"Who?" Ruth said.

"My kid," he said.

"Oh."

"You know the cash register?" he said.

"In what sense?" she said.

He walked over to the counter. "You push this, and then

it opens," he said. "You count. Then you close it back up." He jabbed his finger at the buttons. "Rocket science?" He pointed to the price list. Then he rubbed the inside of her elbow. "You'll be fine," he said, and then, "What's your name again?"

"Ruth," she said, hurt.

"A joke," he said. "Jesus."

When Ruth got home, her mother was making a soup and listening to k.d. lang. Ruth sat down at the table.

"What's that smell?" her mother asked.

"I don't know," Ruth said. She had left her shoes by the door. Her mother sniffed the soup. Ruth flipped through the CD liner notes and looked at all the pictures.

"k.d. really looks like a man these days," Ruth said. "She looks like Johnny Cash."

"I know," Ruth's mother said. "Isn't she handsome? Sometimes I look at her, and I get all confused. You know what I mean?"

"I suppose."

"If I were a lesbian, I'd go for someone like her," Ruth's mother said. She looked as if she were really considering the matter. She stirred the soup.

"Huh," Ruth said.

"Do you ever think you could be a lesbian?" Ruth's mother said.

"No," Ruth said. "Could *you*?"

"No." Ruth's mother pulled the wooden spoon from the pot

and held it to her lips. She frowned. "This soup tastes like the cat's ass," she said.

"I got a job," Ruth said.

"Oh, honey!" Ruth's mother said. "The nursing home?"

"At Nick's."

"Nick's."

"Yeah," Ruth said. "Just for now. Until I figure out stuff."

"Oh," Ruth's mother said. "Honey."

After dinner, Ruth went up to the attic. She lay on her bed listening to a pigeon hurl itself against the wall, sirens approaching and receding. Through the window, the full moon was beautiful as a woman.

She had never had sex with Eddy. After a year, she had come close, once in the back of the cellar near the Solo cups. She had followed him downstairs, the air smelling of cardboard. He grabbed her wrist and chewed on it. He reached behind her and pulled her apron strings free. *You're fucking fourteen*, he said, pulling up her shirt. He bit her nipples. He turned her around, held her head down on the supply shelf, and licked her spine. Then someone started down the stairs, and he pulled her shorts up from her knees and stuffed her bra in his pocket.

She remembered the lazy walk home that day, a new, bright heat in her, something fierce. Birds in the trees. The three crocuses bursting through old snow, and later, cold and white in her fist. The open kitchen door, the ugly silence, her father in the living room, his mouth open and doglike on the rug.

Ruth wouldn't go back to Nick's. Of course she wouldn't. The whole thing was ridiculous. She didn't know what she wanted. She'd always watched others steer their own lives, take action, have strong opinions about things. *You just sit in the backseat.* She seemed to be bad at life, really getting it wrong, like a ferret trying to lay an egg. Perhaps she should go back to Chicago.

She made her way down to the first-floor bathroom. It was dark, and she stuck her hands out in front of her, trying to remember the bones of the house. On her way back up, she passed through the living room. She stood there with the shadows of the furniture. She felt something clammy in the room and sensed that, if she looked down, if she studied the rug too long, right then, her father would be there. Ruth ran upstairs, two by two, and then crawled the rest of the way to the attic, her skin cold and hot as wintergreen.

Every morning, they prepped. Ruth mixed bags of lobster with mayonnaise and mushed it around in a bowl. She poured cocktail sauce into little plastic cups and slid butter between dinner rolls. She shelled pounds of shrimp and pulled the little black ropes from their backs.

"You know that's, like, actual shit," said Mercedes, Eddy's daughter. Everyone called her Mercy. She was the kind of fifteen-year-old that scared Ruth: the eyeliner, the brooding bangs, the pushed-up tits. She painted her nails with Wite-Out. Her boyfriend, Kris, was hanging out in the kitchen. He didn't work there—he just ate. He wore very tight jeans that he could barely walk in and bright white sneakers as big as blimps. He always changed the radio. He liked the kind of music where angry people screamed into the microphone about bitches and banged things. It made Ruth sweat. It made her swallow over and over.

"This music makes me want to die," she said. Her shoes were covered in gray fish sludge.

"Lighten up, Ruth," Kris said. "What's stuck up your ass?"

"Her dickhole husband," Mercy said, wiping her eyes with her shirtsleeves. She was slicing onions in the machine.

"We were never married," Ruth said. She couldn't believe she had told Mercy anything. It was something she had done since she was a child—tell personal things to people she barely knew. It had been a way of making friends.

"What*ever*. Either way, you're *here*."

At lunch, Mercy and Ruth ate veggie burgers at one of the picnic tables out back. They could hear the highway behind the woods. Once in a while a truck drifted over the warning strip and it rang out like hunting season through the trees.

"Are those crickets?" Mercy said. She pointed toward the marsh and sucked on a Camel.

"Peepers," Ruth said.

"Good. Crickets make me think of fucking back-to-school shopping."

It had stormed earlier, and the snails—slugs in mobile homes—were out, painting trails. On the table, cigarette butts lay swollen in a wet ashtray. There were flies all around. The dumpsters were rank as diapers.

A busload of Japanese tourists poured into the parking lot.

Ruth peered at them through the back fence, gnawing indifferently on a pickle. She could feel Mercy studying her. "He looks at you," she said to Ruth.

"Who?"

"My dad," Mercy said. *"Duh."*

"I doubt that," Ruth said.

"What's the deal there?"

"No deal," Ruth said. "We just worked together a long time ago."

"My mom said she caught you guys in the basement going at it."

"We weren't going at anything," Ruth said.

Mercy grinned, then drowned her cigarette in the little tide pool of butts. "I thought it was you."

Inside, Eddy was stressed. Blue piping ran along his neck. He paced in the backroom, slapping his French fry scoop against his apron and swearing. The situation was that the Japanese tour bus ordered forty-seven fish 'n' chips, and Eddy only had enough cut fish for twenty. He punched a corkboard. He wiped his forehead with his sleeve. He brought his bottom teeth to his top lip and frowned. Ruth watched him. She chopped cabbage, shifting her weight from one foot to the other.

Mercy was at the cash register, trying to change minds. "The lobster roll is, like, the tits," Ruth could hear her saying. "Or hamburgers. Classic Americana." Denis, the high school boy who didn't speak, stood by the grill holding a bag of coleslaw and watching water drip from a leak in the ceiling.

"We'll just fucking cut more," Eddy said. He walked toward the fridge, where she was standing. "Move, Legs," he said. She looked at him, startled. He'd called her that nineteen years before. He put a hand below her ribs and one on her lower back, and guided her to the side. He held her like that for a minute, and she glanced at him. His skin had loosened around his jaw and bunched around the eyes. He dropped his hands from her body and walked into the fridge.

"Get a knife," he said when he came out, yanking a cutting board from the drying rack and slamming it onto the table. Ruth pulled one out of the block. "I'll cut and you weigh," he said. "Five ounces." He grabbed a scale, slapped a square of wax paper on it, and set it down in front of her. He pulled out long strips of haddock from a tub and began to cut them on the diagonal. The veined flesh was beautiful and wet, a pink nacre. Eddy and Ruth stood side by side, passing the sections of fish back and forth. He hummed to the radio.

On the last piece, he sliced his thumb to the bone. The fat flared out from the skin. Eddy tried to wrap it in a paper towel, but it bled through and began to drip onto the fish.

"You need stitches," Ruth said.

"Can't," he said. "Don't have insurance." He wrapped his thumb in a dishtowel.

"Christ, Eddy."

"You'll have to do it," he said.

"Are you kidding?"

"Aren't you a fucking nurse?"

"Not that kind!" she said.

"Well, what kind?"

The dishtowel was already red, and Ruth went a little blind. A migraine shot to the front of her head and sat there, like a piece of egg in her eye.

"The phone kind!" she said. "I sat in an office and gave advice for fucking yeast infections!"

"Legs," he said. He grinned, and held his crimson thumb out like a hitchhiker. "Fix the fucking thing, yeah?"

Mercy had a sewing kit in the office.

"Mercy sews?" Ruth asked. Trembling, she put on gloves. She looked for the thinnest needle and held it under a match. She dipped his thumb in a cup of iodine, and then draped his legs with a clean apron. He used to be a fisherman, working with his brothers all the way down to the Georges Bank, until one of them drowned. For a minute, Ruth stared at his hand—his knuckles scarred, the skin honeycombed and red, lined like a map.

She reached for his wrist and turned it over. A long, white gash ran along his palm, trailing out from a bigger mark in the center, like a star with a tail.

"Jesus," she said.

"A beauty, huh? Took a hook in it off Boothbay and got pulled in. Got helicoptered to Boston. My heart stopped cold in the air, and they jumped it back to life." She held the threaded needle now. His thumb was rusted with iodine, and blood was dripping into the apron on his lap. There was more of that egg in her eye now, a whole omelet. She blinked over and over.

"Okay, so—" she said. "So I guess I'll just—"

"You're such a fucking fruit." He took the needle, exhaled, and pressed it into his skin. He bared his teeth and hissed through them. "All right?" he said.

She took the needle from him and tried to steady her hands.

"Want a drink?" he said.

"Sure," she said. "Fine." He stood up and got a bottle from the freezer. He pulled her bottom lip open with his good thumb and tipped the rim to her mouth. A few cold beads of vodka slid down her chin and into her collar.

"I don't live with Mercy's mother, you know."

Ruth swallowed. "Heidi," she said.

"Yeah," he said.

"I remember," she said.

He wiped the vodka from her neck with his hand. "I don't live with any of my kids' mothers."

Ruth pulled the thread through the skin six times. He made her wrap his thumb with duct tape. At the sink, she washed her hands.

"Let's feed a fucking bus," he said, and kicked open the door to the kitchen.

The tourists had taken over the picnic benches and were looking around, staring expectantly at the windows. Children wound the umbrellas up and then down again.

"Way to leave me holding up the roof!" Mercy said, when they came back into the kitchen. Her face was red. "I was about to start stripping! Didn't know if, you know, the Chinese were into that."

"Japanese," Ruth said.

"Yeah."

"I think they would be," Ruth said. "They're into all sorts of stuff. They have brothels where men dress up in diapers and then the prostitutes change them."

"Get *out*," Mercy said.

"Eyeball licking's a thing, too," Ruth said. "I think I read that somewhere. Their sexuality is interesting. They have a very unapologetic—"

"Both of you women," Eddy said, "shut the fuck up."

He breaded and cooked the haddock in bulk, using all four fryolators. He held his hand out as if mid-dance. After he shoveled the fish into baskets, he slid them to Ruth, who stood on the other side of the steel counter, putting them onto trays and handing them out the window. They didn't look at each other, or speak.

After everyone was served, Eddy slammed the CLOSED sign on the window. He took off his baseball hat and ran his hand through his hair. He ripped off his apron and threw it in the hamper. The strings slapped against the canvas. "We're done," he said.

"Fucking A," Mercy said. "I'm gone." Kris was already outside, eating a hot dog and playing with his keys. He was stoned and happy.

"You gonna clean, lady?" Eddy asked Mercy.

"No." She stared at him in a hard squint. Her eyes bounced between Ruth and Eddy. "You kids can do it."

"Go," Eddy said. "Whatever."

"What about me?" said Denis, wiping grease from the grill. Ruth kept forgetting Denis was even there.

"Sure, go, go," Eddy said. "Everybody under eighteen get the fuck out."

Eddy and Ruth wiped down the counters with bleached rags and dumped the rest of the dishes in the sink for the cleaners, who would come later that night. Eddy seemed tense and irritable. He still had to get paper products from the basement and then stock the shelves upstairs. "I can get them," she said to Eddy, who was tucking money in the safe.

The cellar was dark. Steam rasped up the pipes. The air was close and mossy. Water dripped from the ceiling onto the dirt floor. Every few minutes, the generator would burst to life and call out. Through the half window smeared with mud, she could see the occasional shoe, and she heard all the frogs in the marsh, the driving pulse of them.

Ruth heard Eddy upstairs, the slam of the refrigerator door and the wet knock of the mop in a pail. He yelled out the window, "Yeah, we're closed!" and she hoisted herself on one of the supply shelves. The cellar door whinnied open and shut, and as she watched his ankles appear, she reached behind her and pulled the strings of her apron free.

THE PACKAGE DEAL

You know he has a kid, but right now it's whatever. Right now, it—the Kid—is a safe distance from you, far, far away on the remote island called Dad's Just a Rebound. It is early days. If the Boyfriend has the Kid, which is half the week, you don't even talk on the phone until the Kid is asleep. The Kid doesn't know you exist, in this context or any other, and truth be told, you don't ask that much about him, either, but you're not a total ass-hole. You know enough to look pleasant and interested when he talks about him. You learn he plays Little League, which is nice. You learn he gets pancakes on Sundays, also nice. You learn the two of them slouch around in beanbags all weekend, playing video games.

"All weekend?"

"Well, not *all* weekend."

"Are they violent?"

"Violent? No! No. Clowning."

"Clowning with guns?"

"Just silly boy stuff. Father-son bonding."

"Oh," you say. "That's nice."

You have no intention of ever meeting the Kid, so logically you should not be dating the guy in the first place. At the very least, you should wrap this thing up. But it's hard to find the right time when he holds you in his arms and fucks you like that, standing up, no wall. Or when he lays you down, spreads your legs, and takes an hour not touching you at all, just exploring you carefully, telling you how fucking small you are, and how pink, and how beautiful you smell. Or when he puts you in his bed and reads aloud *The Wind in the Willows*, his big arm resting gently on your chest, his elbow near your collarbone, his fingers just beneath the edge of your underpants, until you're falling asleep, until you're falling in love with him.

You tell yourself, "Kid, schmid."

You tell your friends, who ask why you're doing what you're doing, "It's not a big deal."

You tell your mother, who grips your biceps and whispers with soupy eyes that entering a child's life is a very, very big deal, "I know, Mom, Jesus!"

On your first date, the three of you get ice cream and walk the jetty, the ocean swirling against the rocks, cowlicked and pale. You feel anxious and strung out, your tongue thick as a futon, although you've pulled it together somewhat with lipstick and Xanax and long glass earrings. The Kid stumbles ahead, his feet bigger than he's used to, his windbreaker billowing because he refuses to zip up. Besides the bad bowl job from Supercuts, he is objectively good-looking, which means so is his mother.

"Careful!" he yells to you, pointing dramatically to each rock he's just vetted. "That one moves a little!" He has been showing off his knowledge of sports stats, eager to stump his father. "Cy Young career wins?" he shrieks into the wind.

"Three hundred forty-one?" the Boyfriend shouts, discreetly hooking his thumb inside the waistband of your jeans, whispering in your ear that later, when the Kid goes to bed, he's going to get you naked, lay you facedown across his lap, and make you come for his—

"No!" the Kid yells.

"God, I don't—Hey," he says to you, pulling his hand away. He mouths the right answer. "You don't know, do you?"

"Geez," you say, pretending to think. You are so turned on you can barely breathe. "I'm feeling like it's—I'm probably wrong."

"Guess!" the Kid says.

You feign doubt, defeat. "Five hundred eleven?"

The Kid whips around, his lips licked so big and red he looks like your great-aunt Lois. "How did you *do* that?"

"Hey, buddy," you say. "Come here." When he does, you grab the Kid by the hood and pull it over the Kid's head. "I know hoods are crappy," you say. "But having no ears would be crappier." You feel the Boyfriend watching as you zip up the Kid's coat, carefully, so it doesn't snag his chin. You realize how badly you want him to approve of you, to think that you are worthy of his child.

That you would make a good mother.

In the beginning, the Boyfriend is eager to show you their life, and you are eager to show you can fit into that life, and the Kid, thinking you are just a friend, is eager to show off, and in general everyone has a pretty great time.

At the house, the two play PIG with the six-foot Little Tikes plastic basketball hoop in the living room while you watch, hooting, the Boyfriend dedicating each shot to you, the Kid making you kiss the ball for good luck.

At the grocery store, the Boyfriend and Kid make you crawl into the cart, and the two take turns whizzing you down the ice cream aisle.

At night, you watch the Kid's favorite movie, *The Toy* with Richard Pryor, the Kid in the middle of the couch, an arm draped awkwardly around each of your shoulders.

And after four months, eleven movies, one Celtics game, one stomach flu, twelve apple cider donuts, two bloody noses, one Halloween night in which you three are a blender, a toaster, and a pepper grinder, respectively, twenty-three frozen pizzas, and seventeen ice cream cones—which, off-season, the Kid calls "winter cream"—you and the Boyfriend decide to move in together, because you're in love and it's what you do when you're in love.

•   •   •

You look for places on a Kid-Free Weekend. You see one that looks perfect, but the Realtor can only show it on Monday. Monday is a Kid Day.

"Too bad," the Boyfriend says.

"Can't we take him with us?"

"Feels like a lot to ask, dragging him around."

"Don't you want to find a place?"

"Yeah," the Boyfriend says. "You're right." But he looks nervous.

You find half a Victorian with ceilings so high you'd have to stand on the sills to pull down the shades. While the Boyfriend checks out the basement, you explore the rest of the place with the Kid, flipping light switches, opening china cabinets, pretending to look for him—"Kid? Kid, where are you?"—when he runs ahead and closes himself in a closet. You scurry up the stairs and take in the view. "See that blue strip?" you say. "That's the harbor!" You ruffle his hair, and when you put your arm around him, he sort of hugs you back.

"Want to live here?" you say.

"It's cool."

"I think it'll be fun."

"Yeah," he says. "You can visit if you want!"

Downstairs, you corner the Boyfriend in the kitchen.

"He doesn't know."

"Nah, he does."

"So you told him."

"Well, I mean—why else would we be moving?"

You blink at him. "Yes or no."

"Can you cut me some slack? This is—" He sighs a trembling sigh. "I'll go ask him."

"You mean you'll tell him."

"Right," he says. He looks stricken and pale. "That's what I mean."

But later, at dinner, the Kid won't look at you. He pulls all the cheese from his pizza, slowly, and lets it drop like a bloody sock onto his plate.

"He hates me." You're in bed, your heart flapping like a castanet. "Just say it."

"Nope. I asked him."

"That's fucked up."

"What?"

"You asked if he hated me?"

"Yeah. No! I just asked what he thought."

"Of me."

"Yeah."

"What'd he say?"

"He said he likes you."

You think about this.

"What if he'd said he didn't? What would you have done?"

"I don't know," he says. "Nothing."

Moving is difficult, especially when consolidating two households. Extra couches, dining room tables, dish sets—what to do with them? Do they go to Goodwill, and if so, whose? And what about the furniture that stays? There is a clash of taste and style, and you do your best to find places for it all. The living room is a strange shape, and you aren't sure how to arrange the furniture without blocking the bay window. You're working with your couch and his chair, your coffee table, his TV and your TV stand, the antique armoire he picked off a garbage truck. But the balance is off. Maybe it's the lighting. You begin to change the lamps.

"Wait, wait," the Boyfriend says. "I got it!" He goes to his truck and reappears lugging the six-foot Little Tikes plastic basketball hoop, which he places—"Wow," you say, "hmm, not quite sure if that's what I was"—triumphantly in the bay window.

"There!" he says. "I knew something was missing."

On your first Friday night in the new place, you get Chinese and stay up late watching *The Toy*, the Kid in the middle as usual, the Boyfriend's arm along the back of the couch, surreptitiously touching your neck. You feel cozy and happy, excited for your new home and your new little family, and you hit pause and ask if anyone's up for a snack.

"Yeah!" the Boyfriend says.

"Yeah!" the Kid says.

You pop corn the old-school way and serve it in a salad bowl, snowy with salt. You make your mother's Italian hot chocolate and bring it to the boys in matching mugs. The Boyfriend moans as if in a porno. "See this woman here?" he says, swiping his mouth clean with his palm. "This woman is magic."

The Kid takes a cautious sip.

"The best, huh?" the Boyfriend says.

The Kid tosses the cocoa around in his mouth, deliberating, and you wait for the verdict. Your stupid heart pounds. "No offense," he says finally, after an effortful swallow. "But my mom's is better."

"Aww, buddy," the Boyfriend says, winking at you. "That's a nice thing to say about Mom."

Because you are a Man, a Woman, and a Child under the same roof, there is an expectation that you will spend your weekends together. But what should that look like? The Kid, who always seems surprised to find your car still in the driveway, is waiting for another day of Nonstop Fun with Dad to start. Their monogrammed bags are singing out to them, a chorus of beans. There are Pop-Tarts to wolf and footballs to accidentally send soaring into the Rothko print. Later, if they're feeling up to it, they might go to GameStop and blow Dad's money on another video game. If not, there's always laser tag at Laser Quest, a half day at the batting cages, and if Dad has to answer a few work emails, not an issue—the Kid can self-soothe with his PlayStation 4 until they order pizza.

A used bookstore? What's that?

The Boyfriend is stressed. The Kid has already been through a lot. His whole little life—it's too much all at once. But the Boyfriend wants to make everyone happy.

"How about we get you a baseball mitt?"

You play catch in a triangle formation—the Boyfriend

to you, you to the Kid, the Kid to the Boyfriend. You aren't athletic, you never played sports, but you're better than you thought you'd be, and you're stupidly proud, convinced you'll impress the Kid with your mad skills. The day is warm and full of birds. The Boyfriend loves watching you catch, watching you throw, the way your body moves. He keeps giving you that look, the one that says he's going to fuck you the minute he gets a chance.

"Look at her!" the Boyfriend says. "She's an ace!"

"Dad!" the Kid yells, waggling his glove at his father. He does not want to look at you. He does not want you to be an ace. "Back here!"

"Coming at you!" the Boyfriend says, and throws it to the Kid instead of you.

You hold your mitt up, thinking the order has changed and that the Kid will now throw to you and you to the Boyfriend, but the Kid just throws back to the Boyfriend. So the Boyfriend, to keep you in the mix, throws the ball to you, and you, to get the circle going again, make a gesture to the Kid, as if you're about to throw to him, but his back is to you, and he's chipping a hole in the grass with his toe.

One day the Ex-Wife calls the Boyfriend and tells him that it appears all the Kid did last weekend was errands with you. Errands, she says, should be done on the Boyfriend's own time, when he doesn't have the Kid. If he can't put his child first, she says, if he's too busy doing errands with you, he should just give her full custody.

"I thought you said she was normal."

"She is," the Boyfriend says. "Most days."

"So this is one of the other days."

"Don't worry about it."

"Kids can't choose every—I mean, sometimes they just have to do normal—We did other things he liked. Jesus Christ. We went to GameStop!"

"I know," the Boyfriend says.

On a rainy Saturday, you try to make the day fun and cozy. You play hide-and-seek, giving the Kid hints when he can't find the Boyfriend. You make a sheet-and-pillow fort in the living room and serve everyone grilled cheeses in it. Later, you all watch *The Toy*. Twice. When it's over, everyone is glassy and dulled, the Kid sullen. You suggest venturing to the North End for a cannoli, but the Kid doesn't want to. He is moping on the couch, his hands piled existentially on his forehead.

"You okay, buddy?" you say, but he won't answer.

In the kitchen, you ask the Boyfriend if he's sick.

"I don't think so," he says, but he looks distracted and wanders into the living room. You hear a raspberry blown on skin, then laughter, then murmuring. He returns with his jacket on. "We're going to get a cannoli."

"Great!" you say. "I'll grab my—"

"We might go just us."

"Can he stay home alone?"

"Me and him, I mean."

"Oh."

"I think he might need some fun time."

You think about this. "Hasn't the whole day been fun time?"

"Well. Dad time, I guess."

"Oh."

"Look, I don't know," the Boyfriend says. Is he sweating? He seems to be sweating. "How about a nice bath?" He hustles into the bathroom, drops to his knees, starts spraying the tub with cleaner. "There's Epsom salts in a box somewhere," he says, scrubbing wildly, "if you feel like—"

The Kid is standing in the mudroom, bashing the toe of his sneaker into the door.

The Boyfriend drops the brush with a clatter and stands up, flushed. "I'll get you one," he says. "Plain or chocolate chip?"

You shrug. "Plain, I guess."

"Back soon," he says, kissing you on the forehead—"Okay, bud, let's *do* this!"—and then they're gone.

People ask how it's going and you say that everything is great. They ask how the Kid is, and you say, "Nice!"

"Adorable!"

"A riot!"

"You should see the two of them together. He's a mini me!"

You take pictures of the Kid pitching at his Little League games, dancing with your cat, posing in fake mustaches, and you send them to your friends and family, proudly, as if he were your own. You're pretty sure that's how you feel, anyway.

At least you think that's how you should feel.

After work, you look forward to catching up with the Boyfriend with a glass of wine like you usually do. But if it's a Kid Day, when you get home, the two will be in their beanbags on a bed of Dorito crumbs, thumbing their PlayStation 4 controllers, fist-bumping, shouting, *Duuuuuude*-ing. They will be so engrossed they will barely look up.

"What are you guys playing?" you say.

"Sit!" the Boyfriend says, patting his beanbag. "You can sub in for me."

You go to sit down, but then you see the Kid's eyes turn to pink glass. He blinks rapidly and turns his head away.

"Honestly," you say, "I should get dinner going."

"Let's just get a pizza."

"I don't want a pizza," you say, and wander into the kitchen.

You tell yourself, whatever, it's fine, you love to cook, and you can give your mother a call, and you hate those video games, anyway, and this buys the Kid time to be with the Boyfriend, whom, seeing him only half the week, he has missed, and buys you time to be away from the Kid, whom, seeing him at least half the week, you haven't exactly—

Well, *missed* isn't the word you would—

You drink a lot of wine and eat a lot of chips and make a lot of noise with some pots.

"Everything okay?" The Boyfriend has come into the kitchen.

"Yep."

"Pause it, buddy!" he calls out to the Kid. He kisses the side of your neck, under your ear, then grabs two seltzers from the fridge. "Love you," he says.

"Yeah," you say, as he heads back into the living room. "Love you."

While you're not the Kid's mother, you are trying to play the part by, for instance, making the Kid's lunches, and buying groceries for said lunches, and when you do laundry, collecting his clothes from his room and sometimes even stripping his sheets, which you scan warily for whatever, and lugging them down to the basement. And when one morning the Ex-Wife calls the Boyfriend and tells him the Kid has a fever and that this is now the Boyfriend's problem, prompting a vein on the Boyfriend's forehead to bulge thick as a hose because he has to give a presentation to the CEO in ninety minutes, you offer to call into work.

The Boyfriend says it won't happen again.

He says you are a beautiful little miracle.

"Yeah, yeah," you say.

You wait for that Audi to pull up, and when it does, you stand in the doorway and watch the Ex-Wife mash the Kid's face in her breasts as if he's being deployed to Iraq, and as he trudges up the steps, head down, you open the door for him— "Hey, buddy, so sorry you're sick!"—and, not knowing what else to do, wave a friendly wave to the Ex-Wife and call out a friendly "Thank you!" to her cashmere back. You go inside, where the Kid is sprawled on the rug unhappily tossing the remote, and begin to flutter around him, draping the couch with a bottom and top sheet, invitingly folding down a comforter, propping couch pillows behind his normal pillow so the Kid can eat his jasmine rice and still see the TV, and offering him organic ginger ale in the last of your beloved dead grandmother's fancy wineglasses because, you explain, everything tastes better in her wineglass, and later, when he knocks it off the coffee table by accident, you say, on your hands and knees with the dustpan, It's fine, buddy, it's totally fine, he should see all the glass you've broken in your day, really, it could fill a bathtub.

After dinner, you look forward to cuddling with the Boyfriend while you watch TV like you usually do. But if it's a Kid Day, when you get to the living room, the Kid will have beaten you to it and will already be leaning against the Boyfriend with his legs up, happily wiggling his feet. "Here she is!" the Boyfriend says, gazing lovingly and obtusely at you, and you stand there, incredulous, blinking at the Boyfriend's arm slung across the Kid's shoulders, at those toast-colored socks on your pricey white couch, and you opt for the chair in the corner—one of the Boyfriend's contributions to the household, some sentimental wing-back not unlike an upholstered Triscuit—because even though you could technically squeeze in by the Kid's feet, you'd rather sit on a gas station toilet.

You take the Kid to and from school sometimes. On the drive, you turn on the radio and teach him the musicians. If the Kid knows real music, you say, everyone will think he's a badass. This is Heart, you tell him. This is the Stones. This is Led Zeppelin, the Doobie Brothers, Joni Mitchell. Joni Mitchell can be kind of a downer, you say, but she's cool. She tunes her guitar weird. You let him swear, too, anything he wants, and sometimes, when he begs and begs, you drop a new one on him—clusterfuck, bitch-slap, cocksucker—as long as he promises only to use them in your car. And if you pinky swear not to tell anyone—you are the only person who knows, he says—he sometimes talks about the girls he likes, Kelsey and Olivia. Kelsey has dark hair, he says, and Olivia's is lighter, like yours. "Have you ever had crushes?" he says.

"Other than your dad?"

"Yeah."

"Of course."

"Who was the best?"

"You mean the worst?"

"Yeah."

"The guy before your dad."

The Kid's face lights up. "What color was his hair?"

"Brown," you say, pulling up to the curb. "Almost black, like iron."

"Iron," the Kid says, nodding gravely, unbuckling his seatbelt. "Wow."

On Friday, you pick him up after he's been with his mother. "How's Kelsey?" you say. "How's Olivia?"

"I don't know," he says.

"Oh, come on!" you say. You glance at him in the rearview mirror. "Did Kelsey talk to you at lunch today?"

The Kid crosses his arms and stares out the window. "I don't want to tell you," he says. "I only tell my mom."

At bedtime, you look forward to having sex or chatting or doing whatever you usually do in bed at night. But if it's a Kid Day, you will have to wait for the Routine. This is when the Boyfriend follows the Kid upstairs while you wait in bed with your thumb up your ass. You will hear them watching YouTube videos, laughing so hard you can feel it in the walls. A lot of time will pass. It will be late. You will count to ten and back to zero and tell yourself that these rituals predate you, that the Kid loves his dad, that their time together is precious, that he does not want to share it with his dad's girlfriend. Having two parents who are still happily married, you also tell yourself, you can't possibly understand how he feels. He is a good kid. He is eight, and doing his best to adjust, and has had no choice in this matter. In the order of choice, the Boyfriend has enjoyed the most (his first wife, the Kid, his divorce, you), you the second (the Boyfriend, but not the Kid), and the Kid the least (not his parents' divorce and not you). Even on your worst days, you know at least some of the Kid's worst days are worse than yours.

But after another million minutes, you shut off the light and lie in the dark, simmering, and when the Boyfriend comes in, finally, you pretend to be asleep, even when he presses his lips to each shoulder blade, rolls you gently onto your back and takes your nipple in his mouth, and once he has given up and fallen asleep himself, you shove him awake and ask him why he took so fucking long.

"I was putting him down."

"Is he an infant?"

"No."

"Then you weren't putting him down."

"Whatever you want to call it."

"Yeah," you say. "An hour of it."

"I know," the Boyfriend says. "But he likes it."

"I haven't seen you all day."

"What do you mean?" he says. "I got home before you."

The Boyfriend divorced the Ex-Wife for many good reasons, one of them being that she is kind of a cunt, and who, now that they're divorced, is even cuntier and is waging a Spoiling War to Be the Favorite Parent. There are $1,800 laptops, $1,000 cameras, $430 North Face jackets, $250 Nike high tops. There is a playroom appointed with a wide-screen TV, three game consoles, and a Ping-Pong table, not to mention the TV in his room, which is the master bedroom—she took the smaller room down the hall—and the king-size bed. And when she rescues him from your place, in the brand-new Audi *he picked out himself,* he will find his charged iPad and a lollypop the size of a stop sign on the backseat for the seven-minute drive to her house.

What this means for you is that when the Kid comes back, he is shrill and anxious and insatiable, crashing from late nights of TV, writhing on the couch with delirium tremens sans iPad, disconsolate at the reasonable size of his ice cream portions, and the Boyfriend, who finds the Spoiling War contemptible but is unwilling to lose it altogether, appeases him with unlimited video games.

You know it's none of your business. You try to be whatever about it. You try to take deep breaths from your belly like the yoga people.

But the guns.

"Why is that shit in the house?" you say. "Aren't those things rated?"

He looks sheepish. "I was a little out of it, with the divorce."

"They're too violent."

"Okay, okay," he says. "I won't let him get that kind next time."

"But what about all the ones he has now?"

"What am I supposed to do?"

"Get rid of them."

"I can't change his routine on him like that."

"Routine?" You hoot. "You mean his school shooter training?"

He stares at you.

"I appreciate your input," he says coolly. "But I need to handle this my own way."

Kids can be little shits on a good day, even if they're your own. There are the constant grabs for attention—"Dad!" "Dad!" "Dad!" "Dad!" "Dad!" "Dad!" "Dad!" "Dad!" "Dad!" "Dad!"

"Dad!" "Dad!" "Dad!" "Dad!" "Dad!" "Dad!" "Dad!" "Dad!"
"Dad!" "Dad!" "Dad!" "Dad!" "Dad!" "Dad!" "Dad!" "Dad!"
"Dad!" "Dad!" "Dad!" "Dad!" "Dad!" "Dad!" "Dad!" "Dad!"
"Dad!" "Dad!" "Dad!" "Dad!" "Dad!" "Dad!" "Dad!" "Dad!"
"Dad!" "Dad!" "Dad!" "Dad!" "Dad!" "Dad!" "Dad!" "Dad!"
"Dad!" "Dad!" "Dad!" "Dad!" "Dad!" "Dad!" "Dad!" "Dad!"
"Dad!" "Dad!" "Dad!" "Dad!" "Dad!" "Dad!" "Dad!" "Dad!"
"Dad!" "Dad!" "Dad!" "Dad!" "Dad!" "Dad!" "Dad!" "Dad!"
"Dad!" "Dad!" "Dad!" "Dad!" "Dad!" "Dad!" "Dad!" "Dad!"
"Dad!" "Dad!"—the hooflike footfalls, the vinegary socks, the
alley smell of aim-anywhere urine, the plump slugs of tooth-
paste stuck to the side of the sink, the wet towels seeping into
beds or stripping the varnish from dining room chairs, the shirts
used as napkins, the shirts used as Kleenex, the whining, the
moping, the deafening absence of *please* or *thank you*, not to
mention the sensory violation that is mealtime.

But these are not good days.

The kid you are living with is not your own.

And parenting is under the purview of the Boyfriend,
who likes to handle things "his own way," which means not
doing—or even noticing—anything at all. And because you
are not a parent, you have to stay quiet. You can't, for example,
tell the Kid to pull his bangs out of his soup. You can't, also for
example, train him in the Olympic physicality of opening a
dishwasher. When you are crying to the Boyfriend about your
awful day at work, you can't tell the Kid to stuff it when he
interrupts for dessert. Instead, you stand there, sniffling, and
watch the Boyfriend as he vigorously stirs the ice cream into

a stiff swirl, just how the Kid likes it, the Kid leaning over, inspecting the job, and then taking it to the table.

Later, instead, you unload it all on the Boyfriend. The words burst from you, like bats.

"Don't you think he should be saying *thank you*? Seems a little rude and, I don't know, spoiled?"

"His chewing, wow. That's a pretty rough scene."

"Have you noticed he interrupts a lot? Kind of constantly? Tough to have a conversation."

"Does he have to stomp so loud? He shakes the whole house. I mean, is there a reason for it? Maybe there's something wrong with his legs?"

"I'm wondering if he could start carrying his weight a little? Like, I don't know, clear his place at the table? When I was that age, I cleaned the whole—"

"You've got a lot of opinions," he says, getting out of bed with a snap of blankets.

"Well."

"And I'm sure you're right," he says, grabbing his shirt from the floor and pulling it over those pecs, that rippling boxer's back, misstepping and stepping into his shorts, running his hand through his hair, which is wavy and thick and the color of butter, and which you love to hold on to, and also which, because you couldn't keep your mouth shut, it looks like you won't be doing tonight. "But can we limit them to a few a day? I mean, he's my kid."

"Where are you going?"

"I don't know," he says. "I just need a minute."

•   •   •

On Kid Days, you have still been making dinner while they do their thing. But Jesus Christ. You have a full-time job, too, and aren't the only one capable of cooking, and it's not your problem that the Boyfriend is divorced and only sees the Kid half the week. What you'd like is for the Boyfriend to hang out and cook with you like he does when the Kid is at his mother's.

"I'd love to," he says. "But I don't necessarily have an hour to kill in here with you."

"You kill it with him."

"But that's kind of my job."

"He can entertain himself for a bit."

"I can't just leave him in there."

"It's the living room," you say. "It's not a hot car."

"I know," he says. "But it feels funny."

"Didn't you cook with her?"

"That was different."

"How?"

He sighs. "I just think he feels left out."

"Yeah?" You slam down a dishrag. "Join the club."

"Okay," he says. He looks baffled. "But he's just a kid."

You get to the point where the mere sound of car doors slamming in the driveway makes your chest as tight as an asshole. You will have just sat down on the couch with tea and a book when they storm your house, shouting and roughhousing, the Boyfriend, having snapped out of Boyfriend Mode and into

Buddy Mode, now too constrained and preoccupied to kiss you, the Kid dropping his backpack on the floor of the living room you've just tidied and turning on the Play Station 4—"Give her a hug, buddy," the Boyfriend says, before you and the Kid move toward each other, stiffly—and for the next two days—three, if it's the weekend—you pace outside the living room, looking in at them there on those fucking beanbags.

Before Father's Day, you pull the Kid into the kitchen and in your best conspiratorial voice ask him what he'd like to give the Boyfriend.

He thinks about this. "Maybe a new bike?"

"How much cash you got?"

The Kid frowns. "Cake?"

The next morning, you line up the ingredients and drape an apron on the Kid. You have asked the Boyfriend to go to the gym for ninety minutes.

"Ever crack an egg?" The Kid shakes his head. You demonstrate with the first, hand him the second. "Just hit it on the edge."

The Kid whacks the egg and drops it in, all shell. Most of the white slips down the side, onto the counter.

"Decent," you say. "Just pick out those tectonic plates and we'll be in business."

He chases the shells for a while with a spoon.

"They're too quick."

"Use your fingers."

He cringes. "I don't want to touch it."

"Jesus Christ."

You show him how to use the mixer, grease a pan. Everything is half-assed. There is a lot of sighing and slouching and staring, slack-jawed, at the ceiling fan. The floor is a Pollock of batter. For the ten minutes you spend washing dishes, his contribution is to grab the fridge handle, hang from it with both arms, and then let the door swing open with his own weight. "Ow," he says, each time he smashes into the counter. "Ow."

You could kill him.

"Just go," you say.

"You sure?"

"Sure," you say, and within seconds you hear the chirp of the PlayStation 4.

A half hour in, something starts to catch on the bottom of the oven, and the smoke alarm goes off. You wave at the thing with a dishrag, but another one in the living room has started up, too, where the Kid is. You run into the room. "Don't worry!" you shout to the Kid, who has his hands over his ears.

When the rag doesn't work, you try a couch pillow, and when that doesn't work, you grab a kitchen chair and stand on it to take the battery out, but you can't reach the alarm.

"These ceilings!"

"What about that chair?" the Kid yells, pointing to the wingback. He is standing up now.

"I don't think that's any taller!"

"We could stack them!"

"You think?"

The Kid shrugs.

You heave the wingback to the middle of the room and lift the kitchen chair on top of it. You try to climb it, but it's too unstable.

"Can you hold it?" you shout.

The Kid braces himself against the back of the chair and you try again.

You can barely reach the alarm, which, that much closer, is unbearably loud, and you are sweating, and weirdly frightened, and the air around you is only getting thicker, and you realize you never even dealt with what was burning in the first place, and the chair beneath you is shaking, and when you look down, you see the Kid grimacing, his face red in places and white in others, pressing against the chair with all the strength in his little arms, in his whole body, to keep you up.

"Hang in there, buddy!" you shout, and he nods at the backs of your knees, and after what feels like several minutes of trying to free the battery—your ears—you finally whack and whack until the whole thing rips from the ceiling and crashes to the floor.

Silence rushes in.

You leap down from the stack and slap him five.

"Wow," the Kid says, shaking out his arms. His eyes are watering from the noise. "That was badass."

When the Boyfriend gets home, he is grateful, surprised. You sit around the table and give him your cards. The cake looks pretty nice, actually. You cut a big slice for the Boyfriend, the frosting thick as a book.

"Happy Father's Day," you say.

"This looks unreal," the Boyfriend says.

"I made it myself!" the Kid says.

Sometimes the Ex-Wife asks for a change to the schedule, which the Boyfriend grants inevitably and unconditionally, and which you only hear about after the fact. It's your weekend off, but the Ex-Wife has a business trip and has to leave Sunday night.

"So I said I'd just get him on Saturday," the Boyfriend says.

"What the fuck?" you say. "Why'd you give her the whole weekend?"

"I just thought it'd be easier."

"For who?"

"Why are you so jacked up?"

"You're always bending over for her."

"Relax," he says. "She's taking him next week instead."

"When?"

"Tuesday."

You gasp. "But that's a weekday."

"So?"

"That's not a fair trade!"

"Fair trade." He shakes his head. "I don't know," he says. "It's like you don't even want him around."

"No," you say. "But if I had a choice? If I had a choice to be just with you, would I pick it? Sure. Wouldn't anybody?"

The Boyfriend winces. "But it's not just me," he says. He looks suddenly haunted. "We're a package deal."

You start to feel like something's wrong with you.

On the Saturday night the Boyfriend gave away, you put on oldies and pour a bowl of cashews for everyone and a very strong drink for yourself, and you all play Sorry!, whose title move goes like this: upon drawing a Sorry! card, you may take a piece from your Start zone and swap it with someone already on the board, thus sending that player's piece back to his own Start. If one player is on the board, the decision is made for you. If, however, two players are on the board—the Boyfriend, in this case, and the Kid—you must make a choice. This choice should be straightforward—you will sacrifice the player whose position is closest to your Home. But when you dispassionately remove the Kid's piece and replace it with your own, his lip begins to quiver, and he cranks his fists into his eye sockets. When the Boyfriend pulls the same card, it's clear he should sacrifice the Kid, but to control the damage you've done, he pretends to deliberate and, winking, sacrifices you instead, prompting the Kid to raise his head from the table and, his appetite whetted, grab a few cashews, which he pops jubilantly into his mouth. Although your ass is extremely chapped, you feign indifference, because you are an adult, obviously, and also because you can't give him the satisfaction, and so you simply tell him to please consider chewing with his mouth closed. The Kid, meanwhile, having finally come upon a Sorry! card of his own—kissing the card several times and waving it in the air—sends your piece back to Start, not even placing it politely but tossing it at you with something worse than jubilance, even though sacrificing the Boyfriend would have benefited the Kid more, and the Boyfriend was already winning and should have been slowed down instead of pushed closer to a win, and you were already losing significantly, having had only one pathetic piece on the board, the one the Kid sent back. But the Boyfriend pulls another Sorry! card and—aware of your increasing agitation—sacrifices the Kid for the objective reason that the Kid's position benefited the Boyfriend more, which, the Boyfriend explains, is how the game should work, and the Kid, enraged that his father favored you over him, spends the rest of the game taking every possible opportunity to obliterate his father, so engrossed in his vendetta that he does not notice that you are quietly winning, and then have won.

The Boyfriend grins. "Good game," he says, and shakes your hand.

"Seconds!" the Kid says. He will not look at you. He grabs a card from the stack. "Dad, you and me!"

"There's no seconds in Sorry!," you say. You rip the card from his hand so hard you're afraid you'll see blood. "Learn how to lose, dude."

The Kid blinks at you, soggy-eyed, then stomps to his room.

The Boyfriend is looking at you funny. "What?" you say.

He shakes his head. "You're pretty hostile to him."

"I'm not hostile."

"You don't love him."

Love? You don't know what to say. Your heart begins to pound. Your heart is always pounding these days. You fold up the board and tuck it into the box. You collect the pieces into a baggie and pinch it closed. You gather the cards, pat the edges of the stack smooth, and wrap it in a plastic band. The Boyfriend watches you in silence.

"Well, no," you say finally. You tuck the lid of the Sorry! box over the bottom. "Not like you."

The Boyfriend nods. "That's hard for me."

Your face grows hot. "What if I adopted some random kid and brought him home?" you say. "Would you be in love immediately?"

He closes his eyes, as if your very words are too bright. "But he's not random," he says. "He's mine."

"But he's random to me!"

He shakes his head, bewildered.

"I don't think that's my job," you say.

"What is your job?"

"I don't know," you say. "To tolerate him. To be kind, to pack a lunch once in a while, to make sure he doesn't become a rapist."

He blinks at you.

"I like him," you try again, as he pushes back from the table. "I enjoy him. Not all the time, but sometimes."

"Tolerate," he says, heading for the Kid's room. "Listen to you."

•   •   •

When the Kid is over, you start staying out of the house altogether. You spend whole weekends at your sister's or your parents'. You visit friends. Sometimes you just get fucked up at bars alone and flirt with ugly men. When you're gone, the Boyfriend texts you pictures of the Kid because, you guess, he hopes you miss him, or wants you to miss him, or has convinced himself that when you are inevitably beset by a warm, bourbon glow at the sight of the Kid deep-throating a foot long at the county fair, the Kid pointing triumphantly at a golf ball in a hole, the Kid freshly weed-whacked at Supercuts, you will realize you have missed him all along.

Each time a new one rolls in, you look away, stunned and blinking, as if you just got flashed.

One Saturday, the Boyfriend gets called into work, so you tell the Kid to put his bathing suit on. You are going to the beach. "Why?" he says. "It's not even hot."

"Autumn closing in, man. Remember Bob Seger?"

"Who?"

"Hustle," you say, halving a glistening watermelon. "Pretend you're late for baseball."

You carry a chair and he drags a chair and you carry the cooler and he drags the bag and you set up camp at the edge of the wet sand. There are crickets. You play catch with a tennis ball for a while, but you hate catch and you're sick of chasing down the balls you fumble, and after a while you drop into your chair and point to a boy digging a ditch by the water. "Go make friends," you say.

"How?"

You pull a Frisbee from the bag and hand it to him. "Ask him if he wants to play."

"You do it."

"I don't need a friend."

"Me neither."

"Your call," you say, and rest your head back.

You listen to him fidget, sigh, adjust the arms of his chair, pull off its head cushion with a protracted scratch of Velcro, open the cooler and rummage through the food. When you open your eyes, he is looking at you. *"What?"* you say.

"Is there juice?"

"Did you pack any?"

"Ugh," he says, and bangs his head against the chair.

You close your eyes again. "Try to meditate," you say.

"How?"

"Imagine your thoughts as taxis. When one comes, don't get in it. Just let it drive away."

"I don't have any thoughts."

"Then you're ahead of the game."

He is quiet for a minute.

"I'm bored," he says.

"Where's your book?"

"I think I forgot it."

"Sandcastle?"

"I'm not a girl!"

"Jesus Christ," you say, through your teeth. You point to the boy. "Go."

"I'll just sit with you."

"You don't want to."

"I do, too." He pushes out his lips and makes the sideways peace sign of a gangsta. "Look at me," he says, pointing back and forth between you two, his head bobbing as if to a beat, the Boyfriend's old sunglasses low on his nose. "I'm balling."

"Uh-uh," you say. "Go take your balling ass over there."

"What if he says no?"

"Then I'll kill him."

At home, you collapse onto the couch next to the Boyfriend.

"I owe you one," he says.

"How'd it go?" you say.

"Why don't we ever play the lottery?" he says, patting his thighs so you can give him your feet.

"Because we're stupid," you say.

The Kid comes into the room, smelling of hand soap. "What would you do if you won the lottery?" you ask him.

The Kid thinks about this. "I'd get a Mustang."

"What color?" you say.

"Hot blue."

"A hot blue Mustang," you say. "That's it?"

"Yeah," the Kid says. He is watching the Boyfriend press his thumb against your insole, slowly. "And then I'd pay a scientist to make Mom and Dad never die."

"Awww, buddy," the Boyfriend says, patting the cushion beside him. He lifts your feet and slides closer to you, under your legs, all the way to your hips, to make room for the Kid. When the Kid sits, your feet are in his lap, but when you pull your legs in, it's not comfortable—your knees are in your fucking mouth—so you start to get up.

"Stay," the Boyfriend says, his hand tight on your foot.

"There's no room."

"You're fine."

"Can I have one?" the Kid says.

"What?" the Boyfriend says.

"That," he says.

"A massage?"

The Kid nods.

The Boyfriend chuckles, shrugs. "Why not?" he says. He spreads his arms agreeably. "I'll take any and all." The Kid swings around, grinning, and sticks his feet in the Boyfriend's lap, touching yours. You freeze, then watch with horror as the Boyfriend takes the Kid's foot in his hand. "Who says men can't multitask?" he says.

"That's it," you say, ripping your foot away, and storm from the room.

"Get up, buddy," you hear the Boyfriend mutter to the Kid as you stomp into shoes, and then he is coming down the steps, barefoot, to your car, which you are already backing out of the driveway. "Honey!" he calls out.

But you don't stop. You just tear down the street, watching him shrink in the rearview mirror, and wonder when you'll leave him.

•   •   •

When you get home late, drunk, the two are in the living room, watching a movie. The Boyfriend jumps to his feet when you walk in the doorway. The Kid scrambles to hit pause. "Are you hungry?" the Boyfriend says, straightening his shirt.

You point to the Kid. "Why the hell is he still up?" you say. The Kid looks down at the remote.

"We waited to have dinner," the Boyfriend says.

"I didn't want you to."

"Did you eat?"

"No."

His face brightens. "I made pasta." He hustles into the kitchen, motioning for you to follow. You find the table set for three, napkins folded into crisp triangles under the forks, a bowl of spaghetti in the center. There are candles.

"It's overcooked," you say.

He frowns. "How can you tell?"

"It's fucking white."

The Kid has come in, too.

"He did the table," the Boyfriend says. "I mean, I lit the match, but he's the one who thought of—"

"I really don't care," you say, and you close the bathroom door behind you.

When you get out of the shower, the Kid is alone at the table, eating. Candlelight flickers across his face. "Where's your dad?" you say.

"He's on the phone."

"You guys have a romantic dinner?"

The Kid looks down, embarrassed.

"Do you want more?" you say.

"No."

You grab the bowl of pasta and dump the rest of it down the sink. The Kid sits up straight: he's remembered something. "But thank you!" he says.

"Don't talk with your mouth full."

The Kid swallows. "So," he says formally. "How's work?"

"Work?" You look at him funny.

"Yeah."

"I don't know," you say. You grab a broom and start to sweep. "It's work."

The Kid nods.

"Move your feet," you say. He raises his legs so you can sweep under him. "How's school?" you say.

He looks down at his plate. "It's school," he says.

"Something happen?"

He shrugs.

"What?"

"I don't know," he says. "Kelsey always talks to Timmy now."

"That's lame."

"Do you think I'm too short?" he says. "Timmy's taller."

"Nah. Mark Wahlberg's only five-eight."

"Who?"

"A hot actor. Al Pacino's short, too."

"Al Pacino?"

"If you're done, take your plate," you say. He pushes his chair back and grabs his dish with both hands.

"And they're grown men," you say, as he rinses the dish carefully, front and back. "That's as tall as they're going to get. You're just a kid."

The Kid puts the plate in the sink and sighs.

"Dishwasher."

He studies the rack for a while, then sticks it in.

"It's facing the wrong way."

"Huh?"

"The plate," you say. "Flip it around."

"Oh, oh," he says, and fixes it.

"I might be taller than your dad," you say.

"Really?"

"Hard to tell." You sweep the dirt pile into the corner of the room, then lean the broom against the wall. "His posture sucks. He's like an orangutan."

The Kid laughs.

The Boyfriend comes into the kitchen. He tosses his cell phone on the table. "What are you guys laughing about?" he says.

"Who's taller?" you say. "You or me?"

He scoffs. "Is that even a question?"

The Kid claps his hands. "Back to back!" he shouts.

You roll your eyes, then turn around and wait. You feel the warm press of the Boyfriend's shoulders. "No cheating," you say.

"You either."

"Check his heels," you say to the Kid.

"Dad," the Kid says. "I can see that!"

"Don't count his hair either," you say. "It's in his crazy phase. That's an inch at least."

"The term you're looking for is *wind-swept*."

"The windows are shut, Dad!" the Kid says.

"I can feel you straightening," you say.

"So?" the Boyfriend says.

"Stand normal."

"This is normal."

"Stand like an orangutan!" the Kid says.

"Yeah," you say. "Stand like an orangutan."

The Boyfriend pulls away. He looks back and forth between you and the Kid. "This thing is rigged," he says.

"It is not!" the Kid says.

"Fine," the Boyfriend says. He hunches over. "Like this?" He grunts and hoots—*whoo, whoo, whoo, ahhhh, ahhh*—drums his hands on his knees, on the chairs, the candles flickering, and then begins to chase you around the table, his arms low and swinging, grabbing at your ass, the Kid pressed against the wall, squealing with delight—"Watch out!" he yells to you, laughing so hard a thread of snot unspools from his nose— silverware jangling, dirty napkins falling from the table like paper cranes—*whoo, whoo, whoo, whooo, whoo*—the broom crashing to the floor as he comes for you.

THE OFFERING

My fourth-grade teacher, Mrs. Finger, after escorting Paulie DiBona to the principal's office for yelling that she had ass smell, dropped like forty sandbags into her rocking chair and announced that we were getting a paraprofessional.

"A what?" Oeifa Patterson said.

"An aide," Mrs. Finger said, kicking off her stilettos and pinching a few Advils from her pillbox. "The community college just sprang her. Her name's Ms. Jennings. She's going to give me a hand."

Mrs. Finger was built like a mattress, with cashew-colored skin and hair, and was struck daily with back pain so violent she made boys shoulder her like pallbearers to Nurse Eriksson's office. She was a relic of earlier times, before the PTA swelled with professors and psychologists and nonprofit executive directors—the Perfects, my mother called them—parents who nobly sent their children to public school, who made sandwiches with sprouted grain bread and Roquefort cheese, who, against school policy, requested specific teachers, which my mother only learned about after the fact. This explained why all the Roquefort cheese eaters were next door in beautiful twenty-eight-year-old Ms. Week's class, studying the Nile while sitting on bamboo mats and listening to Bach, while on our side of the accordion wall, kids choked down subsidized chicken fingers, hurled the occasional plastic chair through the window, and during story hour tried to pierce their own ears with paperclips. We hadn't gotten to geography yet. All we got for music was Mrs. Finger's labored breathing and the occasional fart blown from the back of the room.

Mrs. Finger invited us to share about our weekends. "Hands," she said.

Raquel Baranek went first. Raquel drank tepid, stinking milk from a thermos all day—this, she told me, was why her cheeks were soft and mine weren't. "I got to ride in an ambulance after my grandmother had a stroke while she was making a bam," she said.

"What's a bam?" someone yelled out.

"I think what Raquel means is a BM," Mrs. Finger said. "As in *bowel*—"

A woman in pigtails and orange corduroy overalls walked into the room pushing a squeaky desk chair. Everyone stared, including Mrs. Finger. She was taller than any man I'd seen, with a long, straight neck and a chin sharp as a garden scoop. At least forty bracelets jangled like house keys on her forearm. We watched her push the chair across the room, a cardboard box of belongings wedged in the seat. She stopped several times to

adjust a tipping Buddha statue and then the straps of her overalls. A few times she burst into silent, wacky laughter.

"Class," Mrs. Finger said. "This is Ms. Jennings. Now who
would like to go next?"

Owen McDonald raised his hand.

"I visited my dad at the Rockingham County Jail," he
began. "I brought him one of my G.I. Joe men to keep him
company. Then he cried and—"

"What's his name?" said Ms. Jennings, who'd begun
unpacking her belongings and arranging them on her desk—a
teapot, a lamp with a red shade, glass jars of nuts and seeds.

Owen looked at her.

"Your father," she said.

"Robby," he whispered.

"Robby what?"

"McDonald."

She rummaged in her box and lit a stick of incense. She
waved it dreamily over her head, murmuring something under
her breath. "That should help," she said, and smiled at Owen.
"Unless he's in for rape."

Mrs. Finger took off her glasses and polished them on the
bottom of her blouse, studying Ms. Jennings. I thought she
was going to say something about the matches, which weren't
allowed in school, or the nail Ms. Jennings had plucked from
her box and begun to hammer zealously into the wall, but she
returned her glasses to her nose. "So your father was crying,"
she said to Owen. "Yes, go on."

•   •   •

When I turned down my street, I saw my father's car parked in front of the house, and I began to sprint up the hill. He was renting a room in the next town over, and I hadn't seen him in weeks. He'd abandoned us, my mother said, because he didn't love us anymore. There were two possible reasons for this, she said. First, he had a brain tumor. Second, he was a pedophile and left the family to protect me. She told me this in her bed, where she made me sleep so she wouldn't be lonely, and where she drank martinis and watched *Dial M for Murder* and all night ground her teeth like a mortar and pestle. Every evening my father called the house and asked for me, but she never let us talk. "We're a team," she'd say, leaving the phone off the cradle. "If he doesn't want to talk to me, you don't want to talk to him." Sometimes she answered and told him to go poke a Bud Light.

I pulled my rabbit, Atticus, out of his cage—my father had given him to me when I was five—and ran into the kitchen. My mother was standing at the sink, smoking a cigarette, her big dream catcher earrings swinging in front of her shoulders every time she took a drag. My father was at the table with his head in one hand and a beer in the other. "Daddy!" I said, and ran to him. His clothes were damp and smelled of old lemons, and his hair was so long he'd begun to shed it like a girl. Stray hairs clung to his favorite shirt—an ugly green thing splashed with bleach stains from cleaning the toilet. My mother had begged him to throw it out over the years, but he'd been wearing it the day I was born and wouldn't part with it, he'd always said, if she gave him a million dollars.

"How about Papa Gino's and a movie?" he said, blinking his eyes over and over and patting Atticus.

"Let's all go!" my mother said.

"Diane."

"What?" she said. "I can't come?"

"Don't do this."

My mother looked at me meaningfully. "If Gretch goes, I go."

He stood up so hard his chair rocked. "I can take my daughter to a damn movie," he said, scratching his scalp irritably with all of his fingertips.

"You can stay for a nice family dinner, is what you can do," she said. She spread her arms. Under her muslin shirt her huge nipples looked this way and that like a cartoon bullfrog. "Your beautiful wife—remember me, the love of your life? I'm right here where you left me."

"Get your coat," he said to me. I clutched Atticus to my chest.

"She wouldn't abandon her own mother," she said. I stared at the floor. "Would you, Gretch?"

"Don't answer that," my father said, and grabbed his keys from the table.

"Where are you going?"

"To get a lawyer," he said, looking helplessly at me, and made for the door.

"Your balls are so small," my mother yelled, hurling a wet sponge at the back of his head, "you could blow them out your own cock!" After he left she came over and pressed my face into her chest, squishing Atticus, who struggled in my arms. "My sweet baby, I can't understand it," she said, kissing my head. "Your own father doesn't want you anymore."

My elementary school was built on a brackish inlet on the New Hampshire coast. While frequently reminded of the privilege of a water view, we played kickball in clay that stank of a litter box, were crapped on by gulls, and ran from bullies wielding blades of sea grass sharper than Wüsthof knives. My best friend, Sally Fantuzzo, had made an alliance overnight with Tammy Zienilski, who was a grade ahead of us and had it out for me. That week they stole my backpack while I was on the monkey bars and threw it over the fence into the marsh. My mother gave me her old pocketbook to use in the meantime. The strap was so long I had to clutch the purse in my arms like a bag of groceries.

The next morning I snuck up to our classroom to avoid recess. Ms. Jennings was sitting at her desk, applying hand cream. She wore checkered stirrup leggings and a wool poncho. Her hair was pulled into a sloppy bun at the top of her head, with stray pieces hanging down her neck and in front of her ears. "I like your style," she said, pointing to the purse.

I shoved it as far under my desk as possible.

"It's good to do something different," she said. "You get noticed. That's what trend watchers look for." I could hear the wet click of lotion in her hands. "Want some?" She held out the bottle and I made my way to her desk. "You seem sad."

"I'm fine," I said.

"Speak your truth," she said. "Last thing this planet needs is another compliant woman."

I told her about Sally and Tammy.

"Are these little whales in our class?" she said.

"No."

"Girls are mean because they feel bad about themselves," she said. "But don't despair. They'll soon enter bitter marriages, become sad eaters, and blow up like porkers."

I looked at the pictures on her desk—cats in windowsills, cats in shopping bags. "Are those your cats?" I said.

"That's Donald," she said, pointing to a fat calico stuffed into a doll dress. "He's my firstborn. Do you have any cats?"

"A rabbit," I said. "His name's Atticus."

"Do you adore him?" she said.

I nodded.

"What's your name?"

"Gretchen," I said.

"Put your hand out." She gave me a tiny squirt of lotion, smaller than a seed. "You don't need much," she said. "It's expensive. I shouldn't be buying it, considering my ridiculous little salary, but I'm turning forty and I mean, really, what can I say?"

"Is it yuppie cream?" I said.

Our town was filling with new money, according to my mother. All of the yuppies, whoever they were, had begun to push out the rest of us. Now the stores for normal people were being replaced by markets where a loaf of bread cost as much as a couch. My mother would get back from the grocery store and say it was too bad she forgot the KY Jelly. I knew KY was fancy, whatever it was—I'd never had that kind of sandwich.

"Yuppie cream!" she said, shrieking with laughter. "Oh, how *perfect*. How *fantastic*. What's your name again?"

"Gretchen," I said.

"I'm Rosalind." The rest of the class was filing in now, hyper and ruddy, hair crazy with salt, mud thick as tires on their sneakers. Mrs. Finger was writing the daily spelling words on the blackboard and telling us to pass in our week's homework. Mine was somewhere at the bottom of the marsh.

"What did you say yesterday," I asked, "when you lit that stick?"

"May whosit be filled with loving kindness, may whosit be well. May whosit be peaceful and at ease, may whosit be happy."

"What's that?"

"The loving-kindness meditation," she said. "Here, I'll write it down." She plucked a flashcard from a stack on her desk, a pen from a ceramic mug. "You can say it about yourself," she said, as she wrote. "Someone you love, someone you don't even know, someone you hate. Always start with yourself."

"Someone you hate?" I said.

"Especially."

"What if you don't hate anyone?"

"You must be unmarried."

"Is it magic?"

She nodded and handed me the card. "Say it three times

apiece. Now go sit down." She pointed to Mrs. Finger, who was coughing up some Marlboro tar. "Looks like Plato's symposium's about to start," she said, and I went back to my seat, cradling the lotion in my palm like a ladybug.

No one could remember a colder winter. Downtown an icicle fell six stories and harpooned a tourist. Dirty piles of snow hulked like bears, so high we couldn't see out our living room windows, and after school kids sledded down them on saucers and into the street. In school we wrote haikus and watered our bean seeds and took timed math quizzes, writing so frantically our pencil tips snapped. We had dictionary races. Mrs. Finger cut blank posters for each member of the class, and we practiced our adjectives by contributing words to each other's like *Evasive! Asinine! Narcotic!* We poured baking soda and vinegar into papier-mâché volcanoes and erupted them onto villages made from driftwood, rose hips, dried cattails, and sand.

All day Rosalind sat in the back of the room with her legs crossed in a languid way, helping students with worksheets, testing them with flashcards. I was never lucky enough to need her help, but I was aware of her—the smell of the musk-and-patchouli blend she dabbed from a little brown bottle onto her wrists, the wind-chime tinkle of her bracelets, and the sudden clatter when, every so often, she shot a hand toward the ceiling and sent the bracelets charging down her arm. Her hands were white, whiter than the rest of her body, and they fluttered around, scribbling arithmetic, dropping soy nuts into her mouth, removing from a Crock-Pot hot washcloths, which she called lavender compresses, and which she wrung out elaborately and then pressed to her mouth. There was the assortment of lip balms, too, layered on with her ring finger, and the eye cream—*two drops for each eye*, she explained to the girls, who stood around her in a circle, rapt, *starting at the inside and moving out*. Then she'd leave the room with her toothbrush and toothpaste.

"Whatcha have toothpaste for?" Raquel asked.

"If you don't brush and floss before and after each meal," Rosalind said, "you'll die young of a heart attack."

Raquel's eyes widened.

"Plus, bad breath—well. No one wants that blasting at you, especially in the sack. Why do you think I divorced my husband?"

"I've never heard of Aim," Oeifa said. "I use Crest."

"Ahh, Crest," Rosalind said. "Procter and Gamble. Do you know what they do to animals?"

Oeifa shrugged.

"I'll bring pictures," she said.

At lunch she chattered while we ate—about her best friend, Penny, whose husband hadn't worked in seven years but his Punjabi eggplant was so good she'd never leave him, and Rosalind's roof, which had to be replaced to the tune of her life's savings, and the deer that came to her yard every night and stared in her bedroom window—"Pervert!"—just as she was getting undressed. She scribbled different versions of her signature on scrap paper and passed them around. "Rank these on a scale of one to five," she said. "I want it to have a kind of erotic intelligence."

"A what?" Sam Dearborne said.

"If each of these signatures was a different woman," she said, "with whom would you have a French affair?"

"That looks good," I said one day, glancing at her Tupper-ware.

"It's all right," Rosalind said. "Kale, white beans, tomatoes, figs, garlic, rosemary."

I opened my lunch box. I'd tried to pack leftover soup in a thermos—my mother didn't wake up until after I left for school—but the cap had loosened and it had spilled everywhere. I slammed the box shut.

Oeifa had seen it. She clapped her fat hands to her face in delight. "Your mom packed you diarrhea!"

"We should all be so lucky," Rosalind said, without glancing up. "Diarrhea is a delicacy on the island of Spitsbergen."

Oeifa stared at her.

"You know what happened to that cow?" she said to Oeifa.

"What cow?"

"The one in your sandwich."

Oeifa looked down at the roast beef in her hands.

"I mean besides dying." Rosalind pointed her fork in the air. "Ripped from its mother as a baby, tail and testicles chopped off—if your sandwich is male, of course. Trucked to slaughter, screaming. Likely crippled. Then dropped alive in boiling water to soften the skin. All so you could have your little lunchy."

Oeifa's face turned the color of her applesauce. "That's a lie," she said.

"Lying is for the uninspired."

"I'm telling my mom."

"Please do," Rosalind said. "It's important to spread awareness." She handed me her Tupperware, still three-quarters full, and her fork. "I'm not hungry," she said, and began to file her nails. "Eat it, or it'll go to waste."

The only time I saw my father was when my mother didn't want to pay for a babysitter. I wished those days would never end. We made lemon cookies and watched the Three Stooges with Atticus propped on a towel between us. Every time Curly went "nyuk, nyuk, nyuk," my father took Atticus's paws and made him clap. We hiked up Mount Agamenticus with binoculars and looked for snow owls, made winter fairy gardens with pinecones and mistletoe, pretended to be Stefano and Georgina, Sicilian hairdressers, and after Atticus, our assistant, offered my dolls tiny cups of espresso, we shampooed their hair in the kitchen sink. When my father ran out of beer, he carried me on his shoulders to the corner store, and I balanced a six-pack on his head as we walked home. Later, my mother would show up smelling of smoke, her features sloppy with gin, and she'd send me to bed, where I listened to her yell until I heard the chainsaw whine of spinning tires as my father liberated his rusted Golf from the icy driveway. I never knew when I'd see him next.

On Valentine's Day, my mother staggered into the house,

lipstick smeared all the way down her chin, clutching two rolls of duct tape. "Do you have to go?" I said to my father. We were in the kitchen, playing rummy and listening to *A Prairie Home Companion*, the impromptu winter jack-o'-lantern he'd carved from an acorn squash glowing next to us on the table. It had two hearts for eyes.

"Of course he doesn't." She came up behind my father and placed her hands on his shoulders. He flinched at her touch. "Let's do a magic trick. I need an assistant."

I volunteered.

First, she said, we were going to tape my father's ankles to the chair.

I looked at my mother.

"Come on," she said, laughing and handing me a roll, and I knelt down next to my father and tentatively wrapped the tape around his jeans and legs of the chair. His socks were browned and had rips along the arches. He didn't say a word.

"Make sure it's tight," she said, the sound of the tape loud as geese as she wrapped his chest and the back of the chair. I looked at my father, but he wouldn't look back. He chewed on his lip with his eyes closed and reached for his beer.

"What trick is this?" I asked my mother as I finished the other ankle.

"A Valentine's Day trick. Now get his wrists."

"What about his arm hair?"

"He's a big boy," my mother said. I tried to pull down his sleeves before taping, but they were too short.

"Don't worry about it," he said.

"Isn't this fun?" she said. When I was finished, she snatched his keys from his pocket. "Now," she said to my father, setting the oven timer. "You have twenty minutes to decide if you still love us."

"You're batshit," he said.

"If you leave before the time is up," she said, "Gretchen and I will have our answer. It's only fair. We have to move on." She motioned for me to follow her into the living room, where she began to whisper. "You're in charge," she said, holding me gently at the back of the neck. "Work your magic." She punched her fists through each coat sleeve and fumbled with her zipper. "We make a great team," she added. Then she walked out the door, got in my father's car, and drove away.

"Your mom's a hoot," my father said when I went back to the kitchen.

"Did I do it too tight?"

He shook his head and gave me a pained smile. "You could be Houdini's assistant."

I asked him if he wanted anything.

"I'm thirsty from all this magic," he said. "How about a sip of that beer?"

I tipped the bottle to his lips. He strained his neck to get the right angle, and beer dripped down the sides of his face and onto his shirt collar. "I'll just finish it off," he said when I took it away, and I returned it to his mouth. When he was done, he told me to brush my teeth and go to bed. I glanced at the timer—there were nine minutes left. "I'll see you soon," he said, his eyes welling with tears. "I love you, do you hear me?"

I brushed my teeth for a long time. When I left the bathroom and looked in at my father, I heard the quiet trickle of water. I realized, after studying the widening puddle under his chair, that he was peeing into his pants and onto the floor. "Daddy?" I said.

"Go to bed, Gretchen," he said, and I ran to my parents' room and lay in bed until, eventually, I heard my mother get home. I would learn later she had driven his car a dozen blocks and abandoned it in a snowbank with the keys locked inside. "Where is it?" my father said, and I heard my mother's maniacal laughter, the rip of tape, the firewood clatter of chair legs breaking against the floor. I turned on a flashlight and studied the card Rosalind had written out for me, her handwriting as delicate as lace. She'd drawn a star at the bottom of the meditation and a note: *Compassion sweetens the heart, RJ.* Rosalind Jennings.

"We'll do an even split," I heard my father say. "I could take her Wednesdays, every weekend, and alternating Fridays."

"She's not getting carted off to some strange apartment."

"Fine," he said. "I'll just get it from a judge."

My mother laughed. "The state doesn't give custody to pedophiles."

It was quiet.

"What did you just say?" my father said.

"She's getting very beautiful. If that's why you left, we understand."

"How low are you planning to go, Diane?"

"She said she doesn't feel safe."

"She did not."

"You wouldn't know. You never see her."

I heard the table move.

"You sick fuck," he said. "Don't do this to her."

"Then come back."

The next afternoon I pretended to need help with math.

"What are you doing here?" Rosalind said when I stepped behind the two Chinese screens she'd set up around her desk. She wore a men's mechanic shirt that said *Bubba* on the front pocket. "You're not a dub."

"What's that painting?" I said, pointing behind her.

"Van Gogh," she said. "Cut off his own ear." She squinted at the worksheet I handed her. "It's a matter of memorization," she said. "Nines are best. You know those?" She grabbed a pencil and paper and began to draw. "Whatever you're multiplying by, take that and subtract it by nine."

"Okay," I said.

"I mean, subtract that number from nine."

I nodded.

"Wait, wait," she said, shaking her head. "Take one *less* from the number you're multiplying it by, and then do all that crap I just said. There's some trick with your knuckles, too, but I don't know that one." She thrust a stack of flashcards at me.

"Is that your cat?" I asked, pointing to her sketch.

Rosalind sighed. "Donald's not eating. I've tried everything. I've tried wet food, I've tried tuna, I've tried chicken and lamb, I've mashed food into a syringe and gagged him with it.

It's not good." She pulled a Kleenex from her sleeve, hard as a fossil, and dabbed it at her eyes. "I love that cat more than I ever loved my ex." She looked out the window at the grubby sky.

"Poor Donald," I said.

"Want some advice?" she said. "Don't save yourself for marriage. That's boarding the bullet train to divorce. Take your boys for a ride. I didn't have that luxury. I was brought up Evangelical, if you can imagine that." She jabbed her tea bag in and out of her mug. "I can count on one hand the number of times that man actually made it worth my while." She pulled the bag out and squeezed it, grimacing. Then she tossed it at the trash and missed. "If I was Captain *Hook* I could count."

I heard Drew yell out, "Faggot!"

"That boy should really consider expanding his repertoire," she said, blowing her nose. She tossed that at the trash, too, and missed again. The floor around the can was littered with fleshy peach pits, seaweed wrappers, old envelopes she'd used to blot her lipstick.

"Drew," I heard Mrs. Finger say. "That's two."

"Of course, there's probably some projection going on there," she muttered. "Best to just let him get that rage out. You couldn't pay me to be nine again." She shook her head in amazement. "When I was nine, I got my period for the first time and bled on the couch by accident. Then Dad came home and tossed gasoline on it." She looked at the flashcards in my hand. "You'd probably rather go blind than look at those," she said. "How about some real cards?"

"Can we?"

"It's math, isn't it? What do you think card counters use?" She took a pack out of her purse. "A woman should always keep cards on hand. My sister and I used to play cribbage every night before bed. Before she became a drug addict, obviously." She shuffled for a while. "Go Fish?" she said, dealing. "I don't want to think too hard. You go first."

"Have any eights?" I said.

"Go fish," she said, and I pulled a card from the pile.

"What's a pedophile?" I asked.

She looked up from her cards, one eyebrow higher than the other. "Where'd you hear that?"

"My mother."

"Can't you ask her?"

I looked down at my lap.

"Oh, boy," she muttered, and drank all of her tea like it was water. "A pedophile," she said slowly, "is an adult who has sex with children. Touches them inappropriately. Or wants to. It's a very serious crime."

I studied my cards.

"Does that ring a bell?" she said.

"No," I said.

"Good."

After a few hands, I heard a knock on the screen. It was Mrs. Finger. "That's quite the math lesson, Ms. Jennings." She frowned at the cards and tapped me on the shoulder. "Back to your seat, please."

•   •   •

On February break Rosalind went to Machu Picchu and came back with a bandage taped to the back of her neck. Before class started she peeled it off to reveal red, greasy skin and a big tattoo. Everyone stood around her while she held her hair up. It was the chakana symbol, she said, the fundamental of the universe.

"What's that mean?" Jeff Maudsley asked.

"Holds the stages of life," she said. "South, for beginnings. West, the darkness of the soul; north, wisdom; east, the place of spirit. The center is a portal of light, to connect us with the pulse of the cosmos."

She told us how she trekked up the mountains with a shaman, ate bark, slept under the stars, woke up suffocating in the middle of the night and was saved when a strange bird flew overhead. She spoke of fifty-ton granite blocks so close together not even a blade of grass could fit between them.

Then she told us about the UFOs.

"Aliens?" the class asked.

"Of course. They've been coming to Peru for centuries. All day, like a Delta terminal."

"Why?"

"To teach us things! How do you think Machu Picchu got built in the first place?"

"Do they come to New Hampshire?" someone called out.

"Certainly," Rosalind said. "But not in peace. They hate Americans."

She handed out worry dolls, which were to be put under our pillows. "You tell them your worries and fears," she said, "and they bear the burden for you. Sounds codependent, if you ask me, but some of you are lugging around some legitimate baggage. Might want to double down and toss two under there."

"That's very kind of you," Mrs. Finger said. "Class, thank Ms. Jennings."

The girls scrutinized their dolls, compared, traded, made little beds and pillows for them with Kleenex. "Dolls are for faggots," Drew said, and ripped mine from my hand and stuck it up his nose.

"Drew!" Mrs. Finger said. "That's two."

Drew pinched his free nostril shut with his finger and shot my doll at Patrick McGinnis's face.

"Young friend," Rosalind said, coming up behind him. "Do you know what happens to boys who stick worry dolls in their orifices?"

He froze. "In their whats?"

"Holes," Rosalind said.

Drew shook his head.

"Skin grows over them permanently. And if the worry dolls feel they aren't taken seriously, they can cast spells of sexual dysfunction."

Mrs. Finger stood up from her desk. "Ms. *Jennings*," she said. "A word, please." She told us to work silently in our journals. Then the two women went into the hall.

"I bet she'll get fired," Oeifa whispered.

"Why?" Raquel said.

"My mom says she's inappropriate. I told her the stuff she

said about my lunch, and she was *incensed*. She even arranged a meeting with the principal."

"What's *incensed*?" Raquel said.

"You don't know?" Oeifa said, and rolled her eyes.

For the rest of the day, Rosalind stayed behind her Chinese screens. She didn't come out when Mrs. Finger started *The BFG*, or at lunchtime, or even for the fire drill. We stood in the parking lot while the firemen lumbered through the building in their heavy suits, and when we filed back into the classroom, Rosalind was scuffing out of the teacher's lounge. "Good fire?" she asked, and disappeared behind her screens until the final bell.

When I got home, I could smell my mother's glue gun. She filled taxidermy molds—hedgehogs, birds, bobcats—with cement and stuck things to them, then arranged them in the front yard for sale. No one ever bought any. Instead, the molds acquired penis tattoos in the night, or got smashed in the street, or were staged mounting each other from behind. She insisted that this art was her full-time job, although my father had quietly suggested over the years that jobs brought in some kind of salary, which, except for the gallon of Friendly's ice cream she won for her third-place showing at the Stratham Fair art show, she had never done.

When I walked into the kitchen, my mother was at the table, fastening marbles to an owl.

"I got you a backpack, dollface," she said, pointing to a pink one on the floor. "You don't have to lug that heinous pocketbook around anymore. I'll always take care of you. Even though your father doesn't love you anymore, I always will."

I stared at the backpack. "Did he call?" I asked.

"Say it back to me," she said. "So I know you heard me."

"I heard you."

"I'd like you to say it."

"Even though Daddy doesn't love me anymore," I whispered, "you always will."

She went back to gluing.

"I hate pink," I said.

"Pink's our favorite color," she said. "Have a seat and let's dish." The glue gun hissed and she rotated the owl, already covered with sea glass, pop-tops, buttons, and coins from different countries. She selected another marble from a bowl on the table. The owl was as ugly as the rest of them. "Are you hungry?" she said.

"Do we have kale?"

"*Kale?*" She stopped gluing and looked at me. "How about a ham and cheese?" She rested the gun on its stand and went to the fridge.

"That pig's testicles were cut off," I said.

"What?" She looked at the bag of cold cuts in her hand. "Testicles—what the hell are you talking about?"

"I'm not hungry," I said, and wandered into the living room to play with Atticus.

When the doorbell rang, I was lying on the rug with my coloring book. Atticus had settled into his towel on the couch and was munching some lettuce. "Yes?" I heard my mother say. I could tell it wasn't my father. Her voice trembled. "Is something wrong?"

I peered around the wall to see a policeman handing my mother a manila package. She held it in her palms like a serving tray. "I don't want it," I heard her say. "This is a mistake." She tried to hand it back. He said something else, and she shook her head. "Please, take this back," she said. "Please." But he was already walking down the stairs.

My mother entered a few minutes later, slowly, her eyes closed. She clutched the package in her hand. "Who was that?" I said, but she didn't answer. She was breathing loudly through her nose and her lip was bleeding. "Mom?" She breathed like that for a while, loud as a bull. Finally, she opened her eyes and looked at Atticus.

"What did I tell you about letting him shit on the couch?"

"He didn't," I said.

"He's unhappy living in a house." She dropped the envelope on the cushion and picked up Atticus, holding him out in front of her. "It was cruel of your father to buy him for you. Rabbits like to be outside, in the fresh air, where they can run free." She walked out of the room, and I followed.

My mother opened the back door and walked down the stairs into the yard in her socks.

"What are you doing?" I asked, running after her. She was walking all the way to the woods behind our house. Sticks cracked like whips under my feet.

"He's miserable in that cage, Gretchy," she said. "I know

you don't want that for him." She knelt down. "He'll be much happier in the forest. It's spring. He probably wants to find a wife." She set him on the hard grass and gave his rump a nudge.

I couldn't move. I couldn't speak or do anything. I just shut my eyes and tried some magic. *May Mom be filled with loving kindness, may she be well. Maybe she be peaceful and at ease, may she be happy. May Mom be filled with loving kindness, may she be well. May she be peaceful and at ease, may she be happy. May Mom be filled with loving kindness, may she be well. May she be peaceful and at—*

"No!" I cried, opening my eyes, but he was already gone.

The next day I failed my spelling test on purpose. "You've gotten nothing but hundreds the whole year," Mrs. Finger said when she called me to her desk. She asked if I needed to see Nurse Eriksson.

"No," I said.

"Go see Ms. Jennings, then." She sent me to the back of the room.

"Even Drew got an eighty-five," Rosalind said when I showed her my test. "And he spelled *faggot* correctly for extra credit."

"What?"

"Ha! Kidding."

I burst into tears.

"Tea," she said abruptly, clapping her thighs. "I have peppermint, Earl Grey, orange. I'm having Earl Grey."

I asked for Earl Grey, too.

"It's caffeinated," she said. "Though, seems like you could use a little buzz. Who couldn't? Wish I had a nip."

She disappeared down the hall and returned with two steaming mugs. "Spill it."

I told her about Atticus.

She listened intently, blowing on her tea.

"And your father?" she said. "What's his take?"

I told her about how he was living in a room downtown, how my mother didn't let me talk to him, how she'd begun to pick me up from school early so he couldn't get to me first.

"When's the last time you saw him?"

"Valentine's Day," I said. "We strapped him to a chair and—"

"Excuse me?"

"In the kitchen," I said. "She set the timer."

"The timer for what?"

I looked down at the table. "To decide if he loved us."

Rosalind stood up and walked to the window, seagulls dive-bombing the kindergarteners outside, plummeting from the roof with such speed it seemed they couldn't fly. She was quiet for a while. "The Incas," she began, finally, "were plagued by natural disasters. Volcanoes, floods, earthquakes. You name it, their crops were ruined, villages flattened."

She paced slowly, those hands of hers, like fancy tea gloves, floating around her as if in water.

"To gain the favor of the gods," she continued, "the people often made sacrifices."

"What's a sacrifice?"

"It's when you give up something you love for a greater good. The Incas were powerless. They didn't know what else to do. So they said good-bye to special things, things they cherished, and made offerings to the gods. In return, they hoped their wishes would be granted."

"Things like what?"

"Food," she said. "Weavings, blood." She looked at me. "Sometimes animals."

"Animals?" I said. "Were they sad?"

She shook her head. "It was believed that where the animals went was far more beautiful than where they'd been living before." Out the window I could see tiny ink spots of buoys, the tip of a sailboat, white as a napkin, inching along the cove. "In some cases they even sacrificed people."

"People?"

"Children, sometimes," she said. "The very, very special ones. The ones they thought the gods would love most."

"What happened to them?"

"They would give the child a feast in her honor, and then bring her to the top of a mountain."

"To do what?" I said.

She looked out the window and sighed. "To never come back."

For my ninth birthday my mother threw a party and invited my father. I looked forward to it all week. She wore a backless dress and walked around the yard in bare feet—it was

the first warm day, the grass still khaki-colored and clammy
from winter. She'd ordered a stained-looking pony who stood
in the empty garden getting wrapped in party streamers and
fed pepperoni and spanked on its butt to giddyap. The girls
at my party weren't friends of mine, really, but daughters of
my mother's friends Sharon and Kit. The three of them sat
around drinking mimosas and crunching on Oriental snack
mix and taking turns ironically French-kissing each other. My
father was late. He didn't come in time for the piñata, which my
mother had hung too high for any of us to reach. She and her
friends had a go at it instead, shrieking with laughter, falling
on each other. He didn't come in time for the presents either,
which no one watched me open because everyone was drunk
or tormenting the pony or crawling around the ground picking
up candy from the piñata, which my mother had eventually
crushed with the broom. And he didn't come in time for the
cake, which was carrot and came from the bakery with a big
rabbit drawn in icing on the top.

"Oh, Gretchy," my mother said mournfully, the rims of her
areolas visible as she bent over to cut the cake. The girls stood
around holding paper plates and pointing to the pieces they
wanted. "I miss Atticus so much, don't you?"

After the cake my mother played her banjo while Sharon
and Kit and their four daughters danced around the pony,
laughing and squealing and sidestepping poop, while I wandered out of the yard and onto the front steps to wait for my
father, who didn't come, not after everyone had left with their
ceramic marble-studded party favors, not after my mother took

a shower and left her dress in a soupy heap on the bathroom floor, not after I had brushed my teeth and got into my mother's bed.

"I know you're disappointed," she said as she wriggled under the covers with her martini. "But you didn't really think he'd come, did you, honey?"

Rosalind wasn't in school the next day. I kept looking at the door, my heart hammering at the sound of footsteps down the hall. We took our spelling test and, in gym, swung on ropes across a poison peanut-butter pit, and after lunch Mrs. Finger read from *The Cricket in Times Square*. For our science lesson we hypothesized that light bulbs had air in them, and when Mrs. Finger cut one under a tub of water with a small saw, the water turned red like when my mother left a tampon in the toilet.

While we wrote in our journals, Mrs. Finger asked three of us—Raquel, Sam, and me—if she could have a word.

"I told you," Oeifa said, smirking, as I capped my markers.

Out in the hall, the three of us stood against the wall. Raquel asked if we were in trouble.

"Of course not," Mrs. Finger said, smiling. "I want to have a little chat about Ms. Jennings."

"Is it Donald?" I said.

"Who?" Mrs. Finger shook her head in confusion. "As you know, Ms. Jennings has been helping us for a while now. You three have spent the most time with her, and I'd like to hear about your experience."

No one said anything.

"I know she's quite the conversationalist," she continued. "Besides math and spelling, what kinds of things does she talk about?"

"Animals are tortured so we can brush our teeth," Sam said. "She showed us pictures."

"Pictures."

"All the bunnies were in cages with no fur."

Raquel sneezed. "Into your elbow, please," Mrs. Finger said. "Well, what else?"

"She," Sam stammered. "She talks about her husband."

"Ex-husband," Raquel said. "That's what you call it when you're divorced."

"Really," Mrs. Finger said. "What has she said about him?"

Raquel shrugged. "He has bad breath in the sack."

"In the—" Mrs. Finger's face reddened. She looked at me. "Gretchen? You're quiet."

I stared at the floor.

"What kinds of things have you two talked about?"

There was nothing left to do. I hoped the gods would love her as much as I did.

"Pedophiles," I said.

"*What?*" Mrs. Finger removed her glasses and absently tugged her blouse loose from her skirt. I stared at the two red seeds her glasses left on each side of her nose. She turned to Raquel and Sam, polishing her lenses. "You may return to your desks," she said. She opened the door for them and waited for it to close. Her voice was lower after they left. "What do you mean exactly?"

I looked at the floor. "She told me all about them," I said, and burst into tears.

Later that day, at recess, Rosalind drove up to the curb, walked into the building, and returned steering her desk chair in front of her, the carton of her belongings spilling when she tried to ease the wheels over the curb. I watched her scoop up her index cards and boxes of tea and jars of nuts and shove them back into the box, wrestle her Van Gogh print into the backseat of her yellow Le Car, the Buddha statue and her lamps, her Crock-Pot—those white hands of hers more beautiful than doves—then slam her door shut and drive up the hill until her car was no bigger than the nail she'd left in the wall. But it didn't work, giving her up. I should have known it wouldn't. I never saw my father again.

EXUMA

Gina wasn't big on kids, but on an individual basis, like dogs, they could be all right. So when she got fired from the nursing home where she was the activities director, she decided to become a nanny while she looked for a new job. She interviewed with mothers and asked to hold the babies: Aidan and Hayden and Braden. She cooed and smiled to her molars. She called them honey bunnies. She asked if they were silly billies. She insisted she didn't mind—*No, really, I love it!*—when they ripped fistfuls of hair from her head.

"I'll certainly read them something," she said, when asked if she liked Dora the Explorer. "I'll keep them safe." Parents liked that she was thirty-four. They liked it very much.

A family in town hired her. The boy was nineteen months. His name was Malachi, which Gina thought was unfortunate. She called him Mallie, and Kye, and sometimes Malocchio, but it was only a joke!

He shrieked all day like a bad oboe, and it made her sweat.

Her left pit always smelled worse than her right: it had since middle school. She lugged him around on her hip, the family collie bursting past her on the stairs, and shakily sang, *"It's okay, it's okay, oh, I know it, it's okay."* He wouldn't quiet, not even when bribed with an extra bottle of warm milk, not even when she tangoed to the "Baby Beluga" song for him and blasted her shin on the dishwasher door, not even when she let him suck on his binky outside of naptime—which, the mother told her, eyes wide with disapproval—risked binky addiction.

The shrieking never stopped. Neither did the lime-colored mucus that sat in his eye like a slug.

Now and then she could get a little loose. Sometimes, when he woke up early from his nap, she didn't go in right away. Not for that long: five minutes, maybe twenty. One day, she grabbed a bottle of vodka from the top of the fridge, shook it like a trophy, and yelled, "Why don't we just have a big drink!"

Once she gave him the finger.

But she was conscientious! She chopped food twice so he wouldn't choke. She wiped the green thing from his eye with warm washcloths. She kept him away from her cell phone, for fear of baby radiation. And on a December noon, after a blizzard, she dressed Malachi in his snowsuit (with two hats!) and put his mittens on (before his jacket so they would stay on better!) and propped him in the blue sled she found in the garage. His parents did not encourage her to take him outside. It was too messy, they said. It was too high-maintenance.

It was good snow, the kind that stuck, blown into swells like a frozen sea. A baby had to see that, Gina thought. A baby had to smell it. She pulled him down the sidewalk and pointed to things: ice on branches, little red berries dropped in the snow, a cross-country skier, a shovel in a bank, a blackbird. When she crossed the street, to Prescott Park, where she would build him a fort, a car scissored around the corner, hurtling toward them sideways. As she tried to yank the sled out of the way, she watched a bit of blue vanish under the bumper.

Two hats did nothing, nothing.

It made sense, Gina thought, that she lived in a house wrapped in ivy. She was a gnome. A forest gnome, living on the third floor. A Bertha Mason forest gnome, with a fire escape. Now, in June, the house was disappearing altogether: just a big leafy thing with double doors.

It was a brick Federalist house, down the street from Strawbery Banke, the settlement from 1650, where volunteer actors walked around in elfin shoes and whisked eggs with sticks. When Gina moved in, she had been excited. She had planned to water the flower boxes each morning through the window, like something out of an opera. She had a bright galley kitchen with a pantry. She had a fireplace and a window seat, perfect for quiet, self-possessed reverie. But the flower boxes just had dirt in them, and she mostly ate soup out of a can, and she wasn't into quiet, self-possessed reverie these days.

She was into TV.

Her friend Joanne came over a lot and watched with her. She worked for the Human Rights Campaign, a nonprofit for marriage equality, and spent her days driving around New

Hampshire, badgering pastors. Joanne was gay, or gayish: she wasn't sure. She liked men fine, but she had begun dating a woman from work. She had sex, she said, but only half of it. She could only receive so far. Couldn't handle giving yet.

"Surprised the ladies aren't banging down your door," Gina said.

Joanne was afraid she'd be bad at it. She wasn't even a good masturbator. Why wasn't she a good masturbator? There was something symbolic about that, she thought, some gross deficit of self-awareness. "I'm working up to it," she kept saying.

"Down, baby," Gina said. "Work down."

After work, Joanne brought ziplock bags of homemade soup and pints of lemon sorbet, which she put in Gina's freezer. She brought movies from the library in tote bags. Sometimes in the bottom was a self-help book or the folded classifieds with a few yellow circles on it.

Once in a while, Joanne drew a bubble bath and made Gina sit in it while she kept her company, painting her toenails on the toilet seat or standing in front of the mirror and studying her hair. "Look at this," she had said last week, pulling at tufts and moaning to herself. "Do you see this?" She took out scissors and began clipping indiscriminately, dropping hunks into the sink. "You know those old wigs with the hanging things here?" She held her fists by her cheeks. "I look like fucking George Washington."

Now they were sitting on the couch passing a sleeve of water crackers back and forth. Gina liked Channel 3, which didn't have any shows except a montage of images from the Seacoast to attract tourists—crabs poking in and out of holes, lighthouses, maple trees. You didn't really watch it. You just had it on.

A lobsterman in waders was tossing traps from his boat, but then the image changed to the shoreline: a mother, a baby squatting to touch a shell.

Joanne lunged for the remote and changed the channel. Jane Fonda from the eighties appeared in a belted leotard. She had a sweat going, walking in place with five-pound weights. She was asking the women behind her if they were ready for buttock tucks.

They watched it for a while in silence.

"The one in the back," Joanne said finally. "That's her step-mother. I think she's younger than Jane."

"Which one?"

"The one with the crazy wedgie. Frontal action. What do you call those?"

"Should I be calling them something?"

"Shit, what was it? Donkey something."

Gina looked at her.

"Or camel—camel toe!"

"*Camel toe.*"

"Yeah," Joanne said. She tried to demonstrate with her hands for a minute. Then she stood up and pulled the elastic of her sweatpants up near her chin. "See?" she said, nodding toward her crotch. "Like a hoof."

Gina chuckled. Joanne was a good friend.

"Thanks," Joanne said, straightening her pants. "Thanks for laughing."

After Joanne left, Gina trudged down to the fish market to buy a six-pack of beer. She drank all of it. Her mother called but Gina didn't answer. She ate Joanne's minestrone and put the rest of it in a pot; there was something terrible about soup in a bag. It made her think of a hospital—of Ringer's solution, of blood. She went to bed and tried not to dream, but did.

Joanne's girlfriend was the manager of the old theater in town, and they needed a projectionist. Gina had worked as one at her college movie theater for a few years after she'd graduated. "This will be good," Joanne said to Gina, who had used up the last of her savings on rent. "You have to get out."

Over the past five years, a board of millionaires had sponsored the hall's restoration and renovation. It had velvet seats and a large rotunda with a mural of cherubs on clouds.

"They recently restored the artwork," Joanne's girlfriend said. Her name was Veronica Messenger, and she wore glasses with green lenses. "It was painted in 1914. Isn't it magnificent?"

"Oh." Gina looked at all the naked babies on the ceiling. She suddenly could not walk, could not do the left and right of it. She would have to wear a floppy hat to work, with a big brim, so she could see only her shoes. Or one of those suits for beekeepers with the metal face shield. She could wear that.

Or she could wear both and then jump off a roof.

"You know, Veronica," she whispered, "I don't think I can work here. I don't even like the movies. I forgot all about that."

"Joanne said you were funny," she said, and motioned for Gina to follow her up the carpeted staircase, which was burgundy and soft. Gina held on to the golden ropes that ran along the walls. She looked at framed pictures of Pavarotti and Sting and Wynton Marsalis. A few retired Nutcracker rat masks hung there, too. At the top of the stairs, people in silver vests were making popcorn behind a counter. They smiled and said hello.

Veronica introduced them: Jerry and Marge. They were volunteers.

"Nice to meet you," Gina said.

The projectionist's booth was on the third floor, behind the balcony. The ceiling dipped, and Gina had to stoop. A large copper padlock hung from the door. "Sorry," Veronica muttered, yanking at it for a second and then fishing in her pocket for a key. "That was Henry's thing. He was the guy before you. He locked it from the inside."

"Really."

"Anyway, the restoration didn't make it this far. Ran out of money."

The projector stood in the center of the room. The booth had a leather chair with wheels. Stained cotton poked through a long rip in the back, as if the cushion had been slashed with a knife.

Veronica showed her how to lace up the projector. "We only have one, so we do an intermission while you change the reel. It's sort of our claim to fame. Increases sales, too, because they liquor up at the bar. Makes a night of it, like a play."

"Smells like Henry was enjoying a few butts in here," Gina said.

"I'm sure he was enjoying lots of things in here," Veronica said. "I'll get that lock off the door and we'll clean the place up a bit."

"It's all right," Gina said. "I don't need anything special."

Each night Gina arrived early and scurried up to the third floor. She threaded the film in long loops and drags like a big sewing machine. Then she sat in her chair, listening to the quick shudder of film, and watched its beam shoot through the rectangular window, a bright tunnel of dust in the dark.

Sometimes, during a showing, she sifted through broken filmstrips that Henry had saved in a shoebox. Time was frozen in a little square, like a postage stamp, laid out for you to consider. If you liked a moment, you could linger there. Otherwise, you could skip over it. You could cut it out with scissors. You could rewind before you got to it. You could pause it and stay forever in the second before, when you were just pointing to a blackbird in the snow.

You could say, *I choose not to watch this fucking movie at all*, and put a lit match to it.

Every Wednesday they showed an oldie. On those nights they gave out black licorice and opened up the balcony, where Gina peered out from her booth. She had begun using Henry's lock on the inside of the door—partly for the novelty of it, partly because she had truly reached gnome status. She decided to embrace the role. Celebrate it. She would wear it like a cloak.

Rear Window was one of her favorites. Grace Kelly had

brought slippers in a compact handbag and Jimmy Stewart was breaking out the telescopic lens. Gina thought about getting one for herself. After all, she had begun opening her blinds.

She saw a woman sidestepping past knees toward the aisle. People were standing up clutching popcorn buckets. Gina recognized Malachi's mother: hair curled in a rock at the neck, shoulders stooped, a smooth little nose. Her husband wasn't with her. Gina remembered hearing he had moved out and was renting a room downtown over the brewery.

Gina ducked and dropped hard onto her knees. She trembled and held her own hand. There was no one else to hold it.

The first reel ended, and the tail flapped as if tied to a bicycle. She rocked on the floor. Five minutes passed, or more. She rocked like that, and rocked. She heard people calling up from the seats. A strong voice was yelling, "Is everything all right in there?" Someone was banging on the other side and jiggling the knob. Henry's lock bounced. The room was silent for a moment. Then the door was suddenly struck, gave way at the top hinge, and spun crashing into the room. A man was groping for switches: the projector, the house lights.

A pair of pointy blue shoes was asking her, Gina, if she needed a tissue or an ambulance or a drink. Hands were on her shoulders, and when she did not speak, they slipped around her, under her knees, across her wing bones—she felt thin and clumsy, sexy as a hat rack—and lifted her up. She was pulled from the booth and carried down the carpeted staircase, her head bumping the wall, her cheek grazing the hanging witch

mask, her long legs emerging from her skirt and dangling—
they were so hairy they could be a man's, Gina realized—over
the golden ropes. She grew hot in the face. "Put me down,
please," she said, pushing at the man's chest, but he only held
tighter and continued to walk. "This is really fucking *bizarre*."

People milling downstairs looked at her, at those legs, perhaps even at her underwear, which, she had absently observed
that morning but was now remembering with acute accuracy,
had a hole that a tiny hedgehog of pubic hair poked through.
The crowd murmured, taking in all that Gina had become, and
parted like water to a prow.

His name was Eric and he looked about forty. He had all his
hair, which was black, and a red beard. His chest was wide,
which made up for the height he did not have, and he whisked
her—he appeared to have whisking *issues*—down the street to
a bar she had never been to, where he called the waitress by
name and ordered two fancy-sounding martinis before they
even sat down.

"I've had them in Exuma," he said.

"Eczema?"

"No, Exuma. Like, you know, *to exhume*."

"Never heard of it."

"They have these colorful fish there that you can swim
with. Parrot fish. They just swim around you. Sometimes you
just can't believe how fucking beautiful the world is. You know
what I mean?"

"No."

"Well," he said. "It's the perfect escape."

They were sitting at their third table. The first one, Eric declared, was too close to the bar and the second had too much light. "You're very particular," Gina had said, padding behind him from booth to booth.

The waitress placed their drinks on the table. "Thank you, my dear," he said. He spoke loudly, with importance. "Let's take good care of our Gina." *Our Gina.* He was an asshole. A whisker, too, a loud one. She would drink her eczema martini quickly, Gina decided, and then crawl out the bathroom window.

Eric was the new president of the theater's board. He said he had worked for fifteen years as an independent producer for Pixar. Now he had lots of money he didn't know what to do with, so he funded things.

"That must be nice for you," Gina said.

"I write these checks, and they want me to show my face. But the movies! It's all incest and abortions these days."

"I like those movies," Gina said hotly. "Those movies are very true to life." She couldn't remember the last time she had been in a restaurant. She felt overexposed and paranoid. Her eyes were sore, shot from too much TV. All around her were Grecian-looking busts of women with hair tied at the neck. They were in the window and on pedestals next to plants. She could not stay in this restaurant. She could not stay in this town. She would move to Fort Myers and live with her mother. She would play Bingo. She would become the youngest Bingo player in Florida. Then she would die. She would ask that her ashes be scattered over something ugly, like a parking lot.

"So *depressing*," he was saying. It seemed he was still talking about the movies and using his hands to do it. They were big hands. They had touched her back and the skin of her legs. "I mean, Christ, I can have a bad day on my own, no problem. I don't need any extra help, you know?"

"Sure," Gina said, drinking with both hands now as if out of a goblet.

"Of course," he said, winking. "You've had a beauty of a day, yourself." She let the wink slide—the man had hauled her hairy legs down the stairs. "You should eat something," he said, holding the menu but not looking at it. He was looking at her. When he blinked, it was catlike, imparting meaning that she couldn't quite interpret.

"I should go," she said. "Thanks for the drink and before with—with the thing."

"Don't go," he said. "You don't have to explain. I get like that during my annual physical. Nothing like a finger up your ass when you're wearing a paper dress. The nurses have to carry me in sometimes."

"Really," Gina said. She stared at him.

"I'm joking!" he said. His teeth were so white they were blue, with an impish gap between the front ones.

"I realize that." She put her drink down hard and it tipped over, breaking. The olive rolled off the table and across the floor like a tiny head.

"Oh, boy, there she goes again," he teased, grabbing a cloth napkin to push the glass into a pile. Gina took one, too, and ducked under the table to wipe up the floor. She looked at Eric's

Shakespearean shoes. "It's just a drink," he was saying from above. "I'll get you another one. I'll get you five!"

"Eric," she said, sitting back up. "You seem to be wearing slippers."

"Slippers?" He lifted his foot up over the table. They were suede and pointy and baby blue. "These are Prada," he said, grinning. "I paid too much for them and they can't get wet."

"That's nice," she said.

He put his leg down and sighed. "Where are you?" he asked. "What can I do?"

"Nothing," she said. "But thank you."

"What if I held your hand?"

"My hand?" she said. "Oh." She set one on the table and looked at it, as if it were something at a yard sale. "That would be all right."

They spent most of the time at Eric's place. He was living at the Wentworth by the Sea, a rambling hotel on New Castle Harbor. Teddy Roosevelt had stayed there once, and the royal family. Eric had been working on a divorce for a few years and hadn't gotten around to finding a real place.

"I've grown to love it," he said. "There's something cozy about coming downstairs for a real dinner. I never had that as a kid. I just made myself cornflakes and cold cuts."

He was staying in the Turret Flag Officer's Suite, in one of the two towers of the hotel. The second floor had a raised canopy bed with a dust ruffle and lots of crimson tassels. Each of the four walls had a little porthole window. The room had a chaise longue, too. "I just sit in it so I can say I sit in a chaise longue," he said. "It's probably from IKEA."

Sometimes Gina let him come to her apartment. He helped with little things: the dust bunnies churning across the floor, big as Ferris wheels ("Down, girls, down!"), her rank sponges, the laundry under the vacuum. Gina had started a pile of it on the bottom of her closet and used that instead of drawers, wearing the same thing over and over, shaking out the wrinkles once in a while, putting deodorant on the outside to make it smell fresh.

"What do you mean, *on the outside*?"

"It's fairly straightforward, Eric," Gina said one late afternoon, a little edgy from watching him flutter around her house in his fancy shoes. She showed him—lifting her arm, dragging the stick across her shirt.

"Oh, the crime!" he cried, and fell dramatically onto the couch. He brought her down to her basement by the hand. "We'll do a sock load first," he said. "We'll start with white ones."

She stood there in her bare feet. The basement was unfinished, with a boulder in the middle of the floor. "I don't think I understand."

"Take all of your socks and put them in here," he said.

"Socks? Oh, no," she said. "I just do it like this." She shoved clothes into the machine. Then she stomped on them with her foot. "Like that. I just put them all in together."

He washed her windows with newspaper and vinegar. He planted begonias in the flower boxes. He even bought a bergamot candle and trimmed the wick for her. "Burns funny, otherwise," he said.

"I didn't know straight men bought candles," she said, sniffing it for a long time. Then she hugged him, the warm animal of him.

She didn't tell him about her past and he never asked. "You were a stray cat stuck in a tree," he liked to say. "You just climbed too high!" He often narrated the story as if she hadn't been there: "And then I was carrying your beautiful body down the stairs, and I had been working out lately, luckily, so I was only sweating a little. Just the pits!"

Sometimes, when Gina was at work, Eric would sit in the balcony. "All the movies look better when you do it," he said. He had screwed the door back into place ("That was pretty manly, if I may say so myself") and brought in an old fashioned fold-up stretcher, which he stuck in the closet, just in case. He thought that was very, very funny. When the movie began to play, he would clap. "That's my Gina!" he'd yell out to no one, his hand happily dawdling in his popcorn.

Afterward, he would stand at the top of the stairs while she closed up the booth, thanking people for coming: "She has such a touch, doesn't she?" he'd ask them. They would smile, confused and slightly alarmed, and push their way down the stairs.

Gina grew to like Eric's tower and its constant sense of occasion: the soaking tub as big as a rowboat, the white-gloved room service, the bleached sheets, changed too often for them to smell of anyone or anything. She spent more and more nights there and left her clothes in the nineteenth-century chifforobe. At night, she peered out the porthole windows at the harbor and could have been anywhere at all.

Joanne came over to the hotel now instead of Gina's apartment. If Eric was around, he'd head to the library to give them privacy. Then he came home hours later bearing takeout and little gift boxes of cannoli, and the three of them played gin rummy.

"You haven't fucked him yet?" Joanne said.

"Do you feel you're in a position to ask me that?" Gina said. Veronica had dumped her.

"Do you even like him?"

"Sure," Gina said.

"The guy's besotted."

"I know."

"I say this with love, Gina," Joanne said, "but I really don't see why."

She would have to sleep with Eric eventually, Gina knew. He had been kind enough not to push it, though she wasn't sure if she should have been grateful or insulted. She sometimes practiced her explanation out loud: "It doesn't do it for me, really."

"I'm celibate."

"I'm emotionally celibate."

"I'm a eunuch."

At the top of the tower, they would lie in Eric's bed. In the dark he touched her body. He dressed the wound of her, attended to things in silence: a nipple, a knee, the soft coin at the bottom of her spine. At times she gave into it, but then her mind wandered somewhere unsafe—to a tiny coffin packed in

snow—and she would turn from him, grateful for the weight
of his arms.

On the last Saturday of October, the theater was having its
annual sponsorship gala. All of the wealthy art appreciators
would be there, with their berets and neutral-colored shawls.
Eric, as the board's president, was in charge of picking the location. He had reserved the Wentworth Banquet Hall downstairs
and had spent an agitated afternoon in his tower, rearrang-
ing the furniture in his boxers. He would push a couch to the
other wall. Then he would stand in the middle of the floor,
eating a package of gummy bears, considering his decision.
Gina watched this process from the bathroom, where she was
filling the tub.

"I liked the couch where it was," she called over the running water.

"It was all wrong," he said, his back to her. "If you sat there
you felt like you were in time-out!"

"You're very busy," she said, lowering herself into the bath.
Sometimes it got so hot in there she thought she was going to
vomit.

"I know," he said. He dragged a wingback chair over by the
gas fireplace. Then he slumped into it. "It's just—what if no one
has a good time? What if people hate the hors d'oeuvres? They
always hate the hors d'oeuvres."

"All you did was reserve the room, Eric," Gina said. "Give
yourself less credit." She had put bubbles in the bath. She liked
that. She also liked to let her hands float in the water. She let

them float like that until she couldn't feel them anymore, but only see them, as if they were mannequin hands.

The party started at six o'clock. At two, Eric left to pick up his suit from the dry cleaners and do a few other errands. "Will you be okay here?" he asked Gina, standing by the door.

"I'll be fine," she said. She was doing a yoga program she had found on TV. She had begun to return to her body a little. It was an old body, tight and dry as a corkboard. She looked at him upside down, framed between her legs, as if he were someone on a postcard.

"You look good like that," he said, a little sadly, and walked out the door.

At four o'clock, Eric rushed in with his suit in a plastic sleeve and a large shopping bag with two gift boxes in it. "Open them," he said. She did. Inside were a black dress and a pair of high heels. "They're just Nine West," he said, pointing to the shoes. "I wanted to get you Prada, but you would have hated them."

Gina held the dress up to her body. It had long sleeves and a simple, sweeping V-neck. "It's beautiful," she said. "How did you pick it out?"

"I had one of the saleswomen help me. I told her you were no-nonsense. 'Gray or black!' I told her. 'She only wears gray or black. She's not showy—I've never seen her look in a mirror!'" His blue teeth shone.

"Thank you for this," she said. "It's very kind."

"Yeah, but will you wear it?" he said, pulling her to him,

grinning. He hummed frantically—something with no melody—and led her in an awkward jig around the bed.

"No," she said finally. "I can't go to that thing. I don't want to be in public."

"Right," he said. "You never want to be in public." He let go of her arms. "Fucking Jesus."

"What?"

He seemed to be thinking. "You really could consider trying once in a while," he said finally.

"Meaning?"

"Try—I don't know! Do you even like me?" He made a face and put up his hands. "I didn't mean that to sound as whiny as it did."

"Of course I like you," Gina said.

"I get hugs. Sometimes I don't even get those."

Gina was quiet.

"I don't know where you are, Gina, but you're not in the world. You need to be in the world."

"Don't tell me where I need to be," she snapped, running down the spiral staircase. Downstairs, she shut herself in the bathroom. There was a little nook for the toilet with a pocket door. She shut herself in that, too. She put the seat down and sat on it. There was a phone on the wall. You couldn't even take a shit anymore without being in the world.

Minutes passed. Gina heard a gentle knock on the outer bathroom door. When she didn't answer, she heard Eric's feet pad away. Then the phone rang. In the small space, it was as loud as a siren. After five rings, she picked it up.

"Gina?"

"What."

"Please come. It would mean a lot to me if you were there."

"It would?"

"Look, I'll tell you what. Come to the party and I'll fly you to Exuma."

"Exuma?"

"Exuma. Remember, with the fish? Tomorrow I'm going to get us two tickets. Forty-eight hours from now you'll be floating in a turquoise sea, numb from a margarita. You won't even remember your name!"

"Oh," she said. She had never liked her name. "That does sound nice." The nook was growing hot and close, like a tomb. A tomb with a toilet, no less. A toilet with a fancy gold handle.

"Everyone needs an escape, Gina," he said.

After she hung up, she sat for a long time. An hour, maybe. Then she pulled back the pocket door. In the larger bathroom she stood in front of the vanity. The sink bowls were copper. There was a stack of small white towels. It was the kind of sink you wanted to wash your hands in just for the sake of it.

So she did.

By the time Gina stepped out of the elevator, she was an hour late to the party. She walked into the banquet hall, where people were milling with drinks and greasy napkins in hand. A long table ran along the back wall with silver serving platters. The hors d'oeuvres had been picked down to the nubs—severed shrimp tails, yellow pepper seeds, felled toothpicks with colored hats. Now people were helping themselves to slices of meat, the ribs of its animal bared and open on the table. It made Gina sick—the hostility of it, the shame. She ate a warm square of cheddar and a few grapes with browning navels. Then she situated herself behind an ice sculpture of the Greek masks of Comedy and Tragedy, popping her heel in and out of her shoe, feeling displaced and panicked, like a penguin on a plane. She looked for Eric but didn't see him anywhere. She smiled at a few people she had never seen before and scanned the room for the booze.

After three glasses of champagne, the roof of her mouth dry-walled with cracker, she finally saw Eric's back. He was talking to a woman with sexy braids—they were messy and relaxed, as if thrown together at a stoplight. She watched them for a while. Gina didn't understand those women, those women who could look good like that. Eric was holding up one foot, showing his blue shoe, and they were laughing.

Braids weren't that great, Gina decided. They were just tails sticking out of your head. It was like saying, *I have two assholes on each side of my head.* She went back to the elevator, to the tower, to the room with the portholes, straight to the IKEA fucking chaise, where she lounged, and where she drank a lot of wine.

"You never came," Eric said, at ten o'clock, draping his suit jacket over the plasma TV. He was in a good mood. Gina was under the covers in her dress and shoes.

"I came," she said. "I came and went."

"You *did*?" he said. "You should have found me!"

"Who was that woman?"

"I have no idea. Was there a woman?"

"Braids."

He thought about that while he took off his tie. "Oh, that was Amy. She's on the board. She's a glassblower. She blows glass."

"Oh," Gina said. "She blows glass." She flipped her pillow and smacked it. "Well, in that case."

Eric turned off the light and got in bed with her. "Can this place make a bed or what?" he whispered, kicking his feet joyfully under the covers. He turned on his side and tried to drape a leg over hers. She felt his foot bump her high heel and then yank back. Then he touched it again, tentatively, and pulled back. She yawned.

"Honey," he whispered. "You got your shoes still on."

"I know that, Eric," she said.

"Oh," he said. He was quiet for a long time. She could feel him studying her in the dark. Seagulls wailed from the roof. "I like it," he said. "I think it's hot."

"Hot," she repeated.

"*Really* hot," he said. He moaned softly and made a show of buffing her shoe with his foot. His leg hair made an animal scratching sound under the sheets.

"No, you don't," she said.

When she woke up, Eric was gone. It was four in the morning. Gina got out of bed and looked around. His suit jacket was no longer on the TV. The closet was open. She looked in all the obvious places for a note—the door, the bathroom sink, on top of her shoes—but couldn't find one anywhere. She could see from the window that his Porsche was missing from its parking spot. She called and called but he didn't answer. She got back in bed and lay there, stiff and alarmed, until the porthole windows whitened with sun.

At ten, Gina ordered a three-egg omelet, an oily beret on a silver platter. She watched a game show where obese people weighed themselves and then clapped ecstatically.

By two, Eric still had not been in touch. Gina called him twelve times, but he didn't answer. She drank three beers and fell asleep.

She woke up an hour later, logy and trembling. She thought about Eric's raucous, solo applause from the balcony, about his quiet humming as he scrubbed her tub, about the way he stroked her fuzzy legs from knee to foot, "with the grain," he called it. And the more she thought about it, the more she felt she could have tried to let him love her.

Or, for Christ's sake, let him do a sock wash. Why hadn't she just let him do a sock wash?

She hadn't had enough socks. Maybe four pairs.

Why didn't she have any socks?

She wanted to raid T.J.Maxx of their argyles and knee-highs, their low-cuts and hiking wools, and run to him, hold them all up in the air—*Wait! I'm here!*—like a woman too late for a train.

Gina took off the dress and draped it on the bed. It was

five o'clock. She put on jeans and a sweater, stuffed the rest of her clothes in a grocery bag, and closed the door of Eric's tower room behind her. On the ground floor, she pulled the outer cage of the old-fashioned elevator open, passed two bellhops with their gloves and silver buttons, and stepped through the main double doors.

It was four miles back to town. The road wrapped along the marsh, with its battlefield of cattails. Gina could see touch-me-nots growing in the reeds. Her hands were cold, everything growing cold now, the seasons always lurching into the next: trees had only half their leaves, and soon it would be winter.

It would be winter again.

Gina walked through a section of woods, where the wind had scattered pine needles across the road. She walked on, over the wooden bridge that sang out, the river churning under her, pushing its striped bass out to sea. There were three bridges to town. On the third, the sky offered up its final strip of light. Across the water, Gina saw the old port, colonial houses clustered together on the hill, the steeple of the North Church.

At the outskirts of town, she smelled fruit burning. Jack-o'-lanterns were lit on stoops. Gina had forgotten about Halloween. It was dark now. Groups of masked children fled up the street, clutching buckets and bags and pillowcases, stumbling up stairs and down again, peering at their loot. There were witches and cats and gypsies. There were pirates and ghosts.

Some porches had cobwebs draped from the roof. Cardboard gravestones slouched in the white grass. Gina heard a cackle come from a haunted house somewhere. As she walked farther into town, she saw the quick flicker and dash of flash-lights across the trees, silhouettes waiting in front doors with bowls of candy in their arms. Everyone was scuffing through the leaves.

As Gina made her way down her street, she saw the dark windows of her apartment up ahead. The ivy had dropped, baring its brick. As she looked, a group of toddlers ran around the corner. They shrieked, darting around her like quick fish, and as Gina sidestepped out of the way, one little skeleton slammed into her legs and collapsed to the ground.

"Oh!" Gina said.

She dropped her bag and stooped to pick up the little boy. "Oh, buddy." She set him on his feet and adjusted the bones on his suit. "Are you hurt?" He shook his head. She held his arms for a moment and looked him over. "Are you?" she said. He shook his head again. The rot of crab apples was thick as a hand towel in her mouth. "What hurts?" She pulled him against her breasts. He puffed short candy corn breaths in her ear. "I tried to get out of the way," she said.

She heard people walking around the corner, laughing. Flashlight beams skimmed the leaves. She clutched the boy. "I'm so sorry," she said into his neck. "I tried to get out of the way!" She held him gently by the sides of his head and looked at his face. "Honey," she said. She was weeping now. "Do you hear me?" The boy began to squirm. *What happened?* Parents were standing around her now, flashlights on her. *Is he all right?* She gripped his little face. "Honey," she whispered, blinking into the light.

LOVE LIKE THAT

Leda would take the train. She hadn't been on one in some time. A few days before, she had read about a woman who killed herself on the track. She just lay there until it came. You never heard of that anymore—it seemed to have gone out of style. She didn't think it was the best way to go, if you found yourself in the business of choosing. Though perhaps it was as good a way as any.

The station was closed. Squirrels ran around and dug up bulbs like little abortionists. The copper rooster on top pointed east, then north. A tall, disheveled man stood near the track with a hamburger, a cigarette stuck like a pin in his lips. He was talking on the phone. Leda couldn't hear much, but she heard him say, "That dog was going to die anyway." He ate and smoked and looked up at the sky. The sun was a worn, yellow slicker. She read the notice on the front door. Due to a bill passed in Congress, Amtrak funds had been cut. She stopped reading after the first sentence.

"Cocksuckers," she said. The Tea Party would burn the whole country down. There would be nothing left: only Bibles and ash. Leda walked back to the car. She would just drive herself.

She glanced at her chin in the rearview mirror. She was growing a fucking goatee—at least this seemed to be the situation. It wasn't the real deal: crabgrass rather than a full lawn. There was a joke—what was it? Something about how Italian men grew beards to look like their mothers. In the glove compartment she kept a pair of tweezers for this very occasion. It took a few tries. She didn't have depth perception, which made some things harder and others impossible. She would never fly a plane, for example. She was terrible at sports with balls and clapping flies dead in the air. Driving at night could also be interesting. She yanked a few hairs out. They were stiff as hay. "Good enough," she said, and started the car.

She was going to visit Jack, her brother. She hadn't been to his place in a few years, because he usually came to see her instead. Jack had some land. He had cows and grew a few things, corn mostly. Also pot. Leda called him from the road. "Train isn't in service," she said. "I'm going to be later than I thought."

"What's that, buddy?" Jack said.

"Or maybe I'll be earlier."

"What?" He could hear fine, but he was frequently distracted. He probably had ADD or ADHD or one of those. He was always doing something else while you were talking to him, and if he was eating, forget about it—eating was a full-body experience, lovemaking of the highest order. Leda was already feeling a little weary of this visit, but she'd be happy to see him once she got there. Plus, Jack was having a hard time. His wife's parents were suing him or something—Jack had a way of accumulating problems—and a visit was due. After that, Leda didn't have much of a plan.

"I'm going to drive," Leda said. "Should be there before lunch."

"Fucking A, Leeds," Jack said. "Fucking A." Everything was always fucking A. Jack reminded her to bear left at the fork—she had a terrible sense of direction—and they hung up. She didn't know how long she was going to stay at Jack's. Maybe a day, maybe two. It made no difference, really. There was no longer a reason to hang around in the event that Mike could steal an hour away.

It was three hours to the house. She paid a dollar at the tolls. The man in the booth looked insulted, as if Leda had assumed he were homeless. She merged onto the highway. As she drove north, the trees grew barer. A tree striptease, she thought. Off to the side, patches of different-colored flowers grew out of the rock like abandoned paint palettes. Her mother was killed on this road. Leda didn't think of it often, but she did now. Of course she had been drunk.

Leda stopped at a grocery store and bought a tub of chocolate-chip ice cream and a box of Cheez-Its. She probably shouldn't have—Jack was on the fat side these days—but he liked them. She also bought some hard, bright apples and a

bottle of wine, and continued down the road, winding through
farmland. A few sheep with new haircuts stood in a field. She
rolled down her window. "Looking sharp, girls!" she called
out. She could hear a woodpecker doing some morning car-
pentry, and all the birds, their picnic chatter. A farmer joggled
around on a red tractor. There were a few casual clouds to the
west. Some things still seemed to be in order—the sky was blue
and the mountains were green and sheep were having some
grass in a field.

Jack's place was looking interesting. Flapping house wrap, window cutouts without windows. Bricks pinned down a blue tarp
on the roof. For stairs, Jack had arranged ascending stacks of
milk crates. The front porch was half-built, the other half pre-
sumably in the grouping of two-by-fours that leaned against
a sawhorse by the barn. A Christmas tree, anemic and brit-
tle, was propped against the fence, a string of colored lights
draped along its bones. Leda pulled into the dirt driveway. She
parked next to Jack's pink truck that, years ago, he had named
"the Vulva." Behind it, a detached trailer full of hay bales was
bowing into the mud. A big rooster stalked a chicken between
two trees. Somewhere a goat screamed so loud, Leda was sure
it was being raped.

   "Hey, hey, hey!" Jack yelled, as Leda warily eyed the milk
crates. He appeared from one of the barns, feet bare, no shirt,
cigarette smoke curling into his hair. He was a big guy, with
competent-looking muscles and a tough, ballooning stomach.
Blood trailed down his legs from where he had scratched fly

bites into scabs. He gave long, suffocating hugs, tight as the womb—today was no different—and his skin was hot and already rusted with sun. He held a small carton of eggs. "Fresh from the cloaca," he said, and grinned.

"The what?"

"You see, Leeds," he said. "In a chicken, there's a consolidation of orifices, if you will. The asshole slash vagina. The vasshole."

"The assina," Leda said, and laughed. She felt dim and far away from everything. Leda handed him the bag of Cheez-Its and ice cream. "For the baby," she said, and smacked him in the gut.

"Fucking A," he said, looking in the bag. He pulled out the ice cream, pried the lid off, and stuck his nose in it appreciatively. Then he tore open the crackers and pulled out a fistful of orange squares. "Thanks, buddy," he said with his mouth full. "Let's enjoy these properly."

They drank some beers on the half porch and passed the box back and forth. *Party-size*, it read. *For the whole family.* "House is coming along," Leda said. "The milk crates are special."

"That's next on the list," he said. He had started renovations years ago, but when he and his wife separated, some things got overlooked. "Got a lot on my plate, you know, with the tobacco plans and everything. Can only do so much in one day."

He was starting a tobacco company. It was his most recent project. He always had a project. He had been talking about this thing for over three years now. It was going to be a gold mine, he always said. Niche clientele. No preservatives, no additives. Not even addictive.

"So there's no nicotine," Leda said.

"Well, Leeds, of course there's nicotine." It was taking some time to get it off the ground, he said. Cigarettes were a harder market than he had anticipated. There were complexities to the thing that he hadn't considered.

"Like cancer?" Leda said.

"That's a little strong, pal, don't you think?"

Jack's brain stored more information than Leda could even conceive of. She learned about the new goat-milk balm all the yuppies were creaming themselves over, about the perfect 30:1 carbon-nitrogen ratio in his compost bins, about the new rooster that appeared out of nowhere one morning and was now hanging out in the barn and boning the hens. He smoked as he talked. He scratched bites, rubbed the blood from old ones, dug at a wart on his heel with a stick. When he finished a cigarette, he rolled another.

"Blow your gold mine over there," Leda said. "It's right in my fucking face."

"Leeds," Jack said. "It doesn't smell. It's organic."

Jack had twenty acres of pasture. Things he had collected over the years leaned against trees and fence posts. Coke signs, washboards, the front of a Model T. Copper kegs, a claw-foot tub full of rainwater. Flowering weeds grew out of an old grain bucket. Jack introduced her to the cows: Brenda and Brinne and Beth. They munched peaceably on some hay. They had silver tags on their ears.

"Does that hurt?" she said.

"Your earrings don't hurt, do they, buddy?" *Pal, buddy.* Leda laughed. She was getting drunk. The sun ducked behind the clouds. A wet, heavy wind blew off the mud. The mountains looked mossy and brushed. She drank her beer.

The cows flicked the frayed ropes of their tails. Flies sat in their eyes, big ones, black beans. They didn't seem to be bothered by it. "Do they blink?" she asked.

"Of course," he said.

Leda watched them, but they didn't do it. She wondered if they blinked at the exact time she did. The thought of this pleased her.

Brenda had apparently given birth two days before. The calf was brown and relaxing on some hay with his feet curled under him—a sixty-pound rutabaga. "Hello, baby," Leda said. "Hello, sweet baby."

"How's it going with Mike?" he asked. They had met a few times.

"I ended it," she said.

He nodded and slapped a fly on his neck. "Good times all around."

Jack forked the hay and filled the water tub. Leda looked around the farm. Rusty carriage wheels, piles of tires. Old trucks in the mud. Jack had lots of trucks. Everywhere you looked was a truck. A toy VW with a red seat was backed onto a stump. Under a tree, a child's plastic table with two chairs was still set meticulously for tea.

"The kids stay with Adrienne?" Leda asked.

"Yeah," he said, filling two white buckets with grain. "She's being a real dick about it." Jack had two daughters, three and five. He and his wife were getting divorced. Leda had always liked her, but who knew what anyone was like in a marriage. Adrienne's parents had hired her a lawyer and bought her a new house. They had also, Leda was fairly certain, cut quite a few checks over the course of the marriage, and now they wanted their money back. They were suing Jack for the farm. Leda knew that her brother would sit in his trailer of hay and light himself on fire before he gave that land away.

"How's the court stuff?" she said.

"I'm doing the pro se thing," he said. "I can take on those donkey cocks myself."

She watched Jack walk through cow shit in his bare feet. "I hope you wear shoes to court," Leda said. She sat in one of the children's chairs. "You need shoes to take on donkey cocks." She finished her beer and set it on the table. She grabbed another out of the cooler Jack had brought down. "Would you like some tea?" she said, in a false British accent. She poured herself a pretend cup. She tipped it to her mouth and made slurping noises. "Today we have Lady Grey. Sweeter than Earl, more delicate."

The cup had a dead bug in it. She placed it back on the saucer. Leda had never met Mike's daughter, but she had seen pictures of her. She was eleven and autistic. Seemed more and more kids were autistic these days, like an epidemic. She wondered what that was about. It probably had something to do with cell phones or Wi-Fi. Mike had been waiting to leave his wife, Alyssa, until Patrice got older, until things got easier, whatever that meant. That had been the plan. Alyssa had never completely coped with the situation and was bad with Patrice—she would lash out and then shut herself in the bathroom for hours—and Mike didn't feel he could break up the marriage. A disruption like that would be at his daughter's expense. Leda understood it must be difficult to be a parent—of any child, typical or not—but Jesus Christ. She didn't know what she'd been thinking, holding out like that. Four years. Affairs were often the downfall of intelligent women. She had read that once in a magazine.

"Got any biscuits?" Jack said. He walked over and squatted on the other chair.

"As a matter of fact, I do," she said, and handed him a piece of bark.

Jack held the bark between his teeth. "Got sick of waiting, huh?" he said.

Running through Jack's pasture was a long gully with an old hickory stump in it. He had been trying to get rid of it for years. He called it the Bastard, the Big Boy. The Blow Job. He had tried everything. He had hollowed it, drilled holes in it, lit it on fire. He had dug down and chopped at the roots. He decided to try to rip the fucker up with the tractor before dark. After, they would do something fun, he said. Smoke a joint at the very least. He wrapped a heavy chain around the stump and then walked to the barn.

While he did this, Leda went back to the house to make some kind of dinner. She saw that rooster walking into the barn. He even walked like a player. She wondered how many women that bird had. At certain points in the day she had felt she was handling the whole thing well, but other times the thought of never seeing Mike again seemed preposterous. Totally unacceptable.

The kitchen was in high disorder. Plywood floors, dangling light bulbs. Sawdust was swept into a pile near the sink. The dishwasher had no door. Leda didn't have much to work with in the fridge. There was a bottle of raw milk with a thick layer of cream on top. There was a jar of chunky peanut butter, opened, with a knife stabbed in it. There was a stack of Swiss cheese on wax paper, the edges orange and hard, and a few knuckled, anxious-looking carrots in a bag. Beer was arranged, head to foot, in both crispers.

She took out a package of ravioli from the freezer and found a can of Italian plum tomatoes. She squeezed the red, wet balloons in her fists. The juice squirted everywhere. Then she poured them in a pot and added some oregano and sugar. She heard the tractor start up. Out the window she could see Jack bouncing over the lumpy pasture toward the gully. While the water boiled, she swept the floor. She scrubbed little worms of gunk around the stove burners and between the tiles above the sink. She emptied the silverware organizer and shook the crumbs from it and then put everything back. She rearranged the glasses cabinet and wrestled the juice stains out of several plastic sippy cups.

It looked like she wouldn't be having any children of her own—she had only wanted them with Mike. She had only ever loved him. Now she wouldn't be having them with him, or anyone else. She was thirty-seven. Not that thirty-seven was the point. She didn't know what the point was. There wasn't one. Maybe that was her problem. She thought about affairs. Flightless, hamster-wheel love. Ghost love. Love on death row. You had no recourse, no rights. Love like that had no rights to anything.

She counted out the ravioli, little cobblestones in sauce. It was important to her that people got their share—she had a thing about that. She and Jack each got twenty-three and a half. Even without garlic, the marinara smelled decent enough. She wasn't hungry or anything, but she had made a meal, at least she had done that. She wondered if Jack had finished his little task yet. It was no wonder, after so many years, that the house was still unfinished. She pictured Adrienne lugging groceries up the milk crates. Leda looked out the window over the sink and saw Jack walking between the barns toward the house. At first she thought he was waving and she waved back. Then she saw that he was covering his face with his hands, which were red. His stomach had red on it, too, and his shorts. By the time she ran out the back door and onto the porch, he had already crumpled into the mud.

At the hospital, Leda sat in a ripe-yellow chair and read about celebrities. It seemed everyone was having a hard go of it.

People were wearing disaster dresses to the Oscars. Some were getting fished out of hotel bathtubs. Others were having meltdowns on Fifth Avenue, running in front of taxis and taking a shit. Leda wandered the halls. In the waiting rooms, people stared wetly at the clock. They exploded into desperate, ragged laughter. They leaned on their knees and swished coffee in their cups. She took the elevator to the cafeteria and ate some forgettable lentil soup. A man at the other end of the table shredded a paper cup. His sandwich was whole and pushed away, his bag of chips unopened. Hours passed. Four, five. She went to the desk and asked for an update, but the surgery was still underway. The nurse who told her this had a silk flower pinned to her smock. She asked if Leda had any errands to do.

"Not really," Leda said.

"There's a good Marshalls after the second lights," the nurse said. "Take a left out of the parking lot." She kept staring at Leda's mouth, a little disdainfully, Leda thought. Her lipstick job was probably not good, outside the lines like a crazy person. Leda didn't care. What difference did it make, really? It didn't make any difference. She had only put it on because her lips were chapped, not because she was trying to look attractive. She did not even want anyone to look at her. The thought of dating again was outrageous. The thought of another man touching her was incomprehensible.

Leda made her way out to her car and pulled onto the road. She drove around for a while until she saw a Kitchen & Company and pulled in. She could get Jack some silverware, she decided, and she could get a set for herself while she was at it.

How you got low on such a thing she didn't know. All her silverware had disappeared. She had two or three forks left, but the prongs were gnarled and sometimes made her stab herself in the lips.

Inside, she wandered around. She looked at all the gadgets. Melon scoops and lemon zesters and garlic presses. She wasn't much of a chef, but she had lots of cookbooks. Sometimes she took them to bed and read them cover to cover. Recipes were like stories, or songs. You could learn a lot about people by the way they cooked their food. It occurred to her that there was no longer anyone to make dinner for. This of course wasn't true—she and Mike had rarely eaten together in the first place. Nights had been off-limits. Weekends, too.

She wondered how Jack was doing. She'd never been under the knife, herself, although she'd heard anesthesia was better than sleep—more like death. She wished he'd never wake up. That wasn't what she meant—of course she wanted him to wake up. When they were kids and Jack was sad, Leda would put on her mother's tap shoes and dance to the Bee Gees until Jack forgot why he'd been crying. She wished she could do that now, the Bee Gees dancing, but obviously those days were over. Anyway, she didn't have the shoes.

She walked down the aisle with the knives. They were all locked away in a glass cabinet. Leda read the labels. COOK'S KNIFE, PARING KNIFE, BREAD KNIFE. She looked at them all. CHEF'S CHOICE, SMITH'S EDGE, WÜSTHOF. A woman pushed her cart toward Leda. She looked carved and wan. She wore a black dress with shoulder pads and clutched a soiled, yellow purse to her chest. The wheels chugged across the tiles. A fat boy in a suit dragged behind her. He wore a purple tie. The poor kid seemed to be off in some way or another. He was plucking tissues from a travel pack. He tossed them into the air, stuffed them down his pants, tucked a few in some oversized martini glasses. He found several purposes for them except to blow his own nose, which was visibly congested and dripping onto his upper lip. By the time he got to the other end of the aisle, he had emptied the entire pack and seemed quite pleased about this. "Knock it off!" the woman hissed. She grabbed his purple tie. "You knock it off!"

Leda walked to the cash registers up front. A woman behind the desk was putting wineglasses in a bag and tucking them in with brown paper. She attended to them intensely, as a child would with dolls. Leda almost expected her to pull out a baby bottle, but of course she didn't. Leda watched her for a moment. She had cherries painted on her pointer fingers. Her nametag said *Juliet 3 Yrs.* "Do you have stainless steel?" Leda asked, finally.

The woman looked up. She stopped tucking to consider this. "Like, appliances?"

Leda knew stainless steel wasn't what she meant, but all of a sudden she couldn't recall the word. "No, I mean—" Leda thought for a minute. "You know, like, stuff you eat with."

The woman stared at her. She looked scared, and Leda couldn't blame her. "I'm not sure—"

"You know," Leda said. She demonstrated with her hands. She brought them to her mouth in a shoveling motion and began to pretend chew. She couldn't recall the word, not for anything. If someone had a gun and said, *I will shoot you if you don't think of the word for the things you eat with,* she would have been fucked—more so, in fact, as she could not think under pressure. "Oh, come on," she said, a little maniacally. "You know!"

"Like, forks?" the woman said.

"Forks!" Leda said. "Forks!"

"Silverware."

"Wow," Leda said. "There it is. Do you have that?"

She bought two sets on sale. They weren't anything fancy, but they would get the job done. She put the shopping bag in the backseat and drove back to the hospital.

In the waiting room, she doodled on a napkin. She drew a man with no eyes. She gave him a tail. She gave him a mouth, too, but it came out wrong. She changed it into a flower. The pen was a nice one. *This is a pretty nice pen,* she wrote. There was a jar of them on the coffee table. She took two and put them in her purse. The surgeon came out for the report. He was an eye specialist called in from somewhere else. A paper mask hung from one ear. He waved her into the hall. "As you know, the chain your brother was using to pull out the tree stump snapped and skimmed his face."

She stared at him. "Okay," she said.

"To be honest, I don't know how he is alive."

"Okay."

"Both eyes have sustained severe trauma." He looked angry. She wondered if perhaps he had seen her take the pens, but of course that was ridiculous. It was two a.m. and she realized, at once, that she was very tired, the fatigue in her blurring and bright gray. She remembered waking up on the kitchen floor and then driving to the train station. She leaned against a hand sanitizer. Everywhere there was a hand sanitizer.

"What did you say?" she said.

"The left eye was split in two. We stitched it up. We'll discuss prosthesis options if that is something that interests him."

"What about the other one?"

"There's too much swelling to know the big picture conclusively."

"But it's still there."

"Yes."

"What's the little picture?"

"Eye drops, medication. He'll need round-the-clock care."

"Will he see out of the other one? The one you stitched?"

"I have little hope for it."

"Does he have to know that?"

Leda didn't actually know what she was looking at. The right eye was a red, ballooning thing. The left looked like a piece of intestine. A nurse showed Leda how to administer the drops. There were seven different kinds.

"You okay doing that, Leeds?" Jack said.

"Of course," she said. Then she excused herself to the bathroom. She put her hands over her eyes. She pretended she couldn't take them off. She wondered if the darkness at the back of her lids was the same as having no eyes at all. She remembered a doll she had had as a child, her favorite doll. One day the dog had mauled it and bitten its eyes out. Her mother had taped some marbles in their place—she had tried in her own inept way, Leda supposed—but after that it wasn't the same. She thought she was going to be sick. She huddled over the toilet, but nothing happened.

When she came out, the nurse was replacing the bandages. There was hay in Jack's hair. There was dried blood on his forearms and chin. She wiped at these with a washcloth after the nurse left the room. "Clean yourself up, for Christ's sake," she joked.

"Good times, huh, Leeds?" he said.

He didn't have insurance. He didn't want to stay another night. Plus, Jack said, someone had to get back to feed the cows. They were probably walking down to a restaurant by now, he said. Out in the hall by the elevator, Leda called Adrienne. She was sorry to hear about the accident, she said. It was terrible. Everyone knew something like this had been coming. She felt for him—she did. Jack would have to hire help, she said. Or just sell the fucking farm. If he had done that to begin with, she said, this never would have happened. If he sold it, it would save him a lot of trouble down the line. She was not going to let the kids go over and see him like that, if that's what Leda was thinking. If that's what Leda was thinking, she must be crazy.

"You're really something," Leda said, and hung up.

She drove Jack home. It began to rain. Jack didn't have any shoes, of course. He hadn't had a shirt, either, but the hospital had given him a giant pink smock. He leaned against the headrest.

"It's raining, huh?" he said.

"A little." She saw a tear drip out from under his right bandage. Leda stopped at the pharmacy to pick up his prescriptions. "Wait here," she said, not that he was going anywhere. There were ten prescriptions. Each time the man handed her another one, she had to sign on the line.

"Do you have any questions for the pharmacist?" he said.

"No."

She bought Jack some sunglasses. Back in the car, she handed them to him.

"They don't make me look blind, do they?" he said. "Are these old man wraparounds?"

"Would I buy those?" Leda said.

They continued home. She squinted at the road. She imagined Mike eating breakfast with Alyssa and Patrice. She wondered how he was managing. Last she had seen him, he was sitting on the grass at the park, crying into his hands. *You don't understand it,* he had said. *She's my child. What am I supposed to do?*

She kept braking for animals in the road, but there was nothing there. "You just learn to drive, Leeds?" he said. "You'll lower your gas mileage like that."

She helped him up the milk crates. He wrapped his arm around her shoulders. She wrapped both of hers around his torso. "Two more," she said. "One more." She turned on the lights and guided him into a kitchen chair. The two plates of ravioli were still there and a pot of marinara on a coaster. The ladle was on the doormat in a small patty of dried sauce. The window over the sink was open. Receipts and napkins blew around the kitchen floor. It was cold inside. She shut the window and looked for the thermostat, but there wasn't one. "How do you turn on the heat?" she said.

"Woodstove, buddy," he said. He sat on the couch and walked her through it. Rings of twisted newspaper, cardboard. Big kindling, small kindling. Tepee effect for maximum air circulation. "Did you make the tepee?" he said. "Make the tepee, pal."

"Tepee, okay," she said. "Tepee."

She made a spreadsheet for the drops and meds. She used highlighters and drew stars and arrows everywhere. It was all very confusing. She went outside and forked the hay. The buckets were heavy, and she had to keep stopping to put them down.

He tried to call his kids, but no one answered. "Maybe they're out," Leda suggested.

She helped him take a bath. He wore his boxer shorts in the tub. They were blue with lobsters on them. She pushed the hot water past his hips. She folded a towel and knelt on it. She scrubbed mud from his elbows. She cupped her hand on his forehead and poured a sippy cup of water down the back of his head. She filled and poured, filled and poured. The faucet dripped. The tiles had scabbed off and the shower curtain was ripped and gray with mold. His shaving can had left circles of rust on the tub. There was still a basket of bath toys on the floor. Foam letters, plastic whales. Boats.

"Is it too hot?" she said.

"No."

"Is it hot enough?"

His penis slumped out of his shorts.

"You're falling out, sort of," she said.

"What?" he said. His knees stuck out of the tub. Dark bruises were taking over his cheekbone and nose.

"Your thing," she said. "Your little—"

He pushed it back in his shorts.

"Little?" he said.

She added more hot water.

"Not *little* little," she said. "Just, you know. Low-key little."

"Thanks, pal," he said.

"What are you going to name that baby cow?" she asked him. Buster, maybe, or Babar. Buddy.

"Nothing," he said. "He's a bull. He'll go to a cattle farm."

"Does he have to?"

Downstairs, she set Jack up on the couch with pillows and a checkered comforter. "How about some TV?" she said. "Want to watch *Star Wars*?"

"*Watch?*"

"Or we can read a book together. I'll make hot chocolate and popcorn. We'll have a book festival. We'll read every goddamn book you want."

"Fuck, Leeds," he said, and she looked over at him under the blanket. She could still see him when he was ten—knees scabbed, teeth bucked. Home alone washing the dishes, their father long gone, their mother waiting tables at Cindy's Place, bringing home Ron or Don or Dutch and getting felt up in the family room. Leda had come back from college every Wednesday night and weekend, as often as she could. She made him lunches three days in advance. She double-checked his math homework. When he couldn't figure it out, she just told him the answers.

"I know," she said.

She started *David Copperfield*. She read it intensely and with animation. She gave all the characters different voices. Sometimes she got them confused. Sometimes Tommy Traddles sounded a lot like Peggotty. Once in a while, her British accent got a little out of hand. Sometimes Davy sounded like a Texan, or a drag queen. She kept reading. She consulted her spreadsheet, shoved a log in the stove, slow-cooked a sauce, arranged the Kitchen & Company silverware in his drawer. She called HR and worked something out.

Weeks passed. She kept reading. They drank hot chocolate. They ate popcorn out of a yellow bowl.

PLAGIARISM

It wasn't even lunch yet, and Helen had a plagiarism situation on her hands. Becky Fairchild: chipper with lots of teeth, field hockey captain, hair ribbons of Hadley Academy colors every Friday, scones and effusive thank-you notes for teachers at Christmas, clothes from the kind of catalogs that Helen flipped through wistfully while on the toilet. Becky truly was not bright. During class discussion, she brandished a lint-roller from her backpack and ran it dreamily over her breasts, and when called on volunteered others for the job—"Why doesn't Richard tell us what *he* thinks!" When you got down to it, the only time she had anything to say was when she delivered her daily appraisal of Helen's outfit from the back of the room—"Jeans, wow. Ms. Fiore's not wearing her usual skirt!" or "Ms. Fiore, you're looking so *bohemian* today with that crazy *scarf*"—so relentlessly that, while Tim still slept, it was Becky Helen found herself anxiously dressing for each morning, wondering if she'd meant *crazy* in a bad way.

And now Becky, overnight, had turned into an expert on devotional imagery in *Jane Eyre*. After ten minutes online, Helen found the source: an essay in *Brontë Studies*. How the girl had known such a journal existed was a different question entirely. Her father must have helped her.

But all kids had something beautiful and redeeming about them. Sometimes you just had to look a little harder and wait for that beautiful and redeeming something to present itself. Like when Matt Hoffstat had gestured in a very sweet and discreet way about the parsley in Helen's teeth. She had never forgotten it. In fact, she made a mental note to send Matt a letter in prison and let him know people were thinking about him. Or what the hell, just drive down there and say hello! Tragic how a life could explode. One minute it was tubby time and *Stuart Little* and the next you were setting fire to a nursing home. Though she doubted Matt had had any *Stuart Little*. Helen certainly hadn't. One look at Matt's father, frankly, and Helen could understand how someone might just lose it and feel that setting a nursing home on fire was actually the only reasonable thing one *could* do. Or not *understand*, of course, but—

Point was, now Helen had to be mean: write Becky up, meet with the headmaster, call the parents. And during School Spirit Week. That was the worst of it. Each day everyone was supposed to dress in a different theme: Favorite Food Day, Favorite TV Character Day, Opposite Sex Day (great, really sensitive, with poor Oliver-turned-Olivia recently sporting his—her! her!—new gel bras). Today, Thursday, was Clash Day.

Becky wore jeans under a dress, stripes over plaid, knee socks, a man's tie in a loose knot, a flip-flop and a high heel, yellow oven mitts on both hands.

"You can't possibly expect me to take a *test* like *this*!" she'd said gleefully, mitts to the overhead lights.

What was Helen supposed to do, call her out dressed like that? It was bad enough to be caught for the Big P, the rape of academe, but to be yelled at—no. You didn't yell. Worse than that, you stepped in the hall and murmured. She could see it all now: the censure, the funereal loss of faith, the ugly paperwork, all while Becky was dressed like a clown.

Horrible.

Helen took a red pen and wrote on the last page: *I cannot accept this essay.* Then added: *Let's chat.* Seemed friendlier. She'd talk to Ron, the headmaster, tomorrow.

In the teachers' lounge Helen's friend Peg (pre-calculus) was studying the microwave like a child at a terrarium, opening the door every twenty seconds to poke at her macaroni and cheese.

"Better cover those tits if you're going to stand that close," said Paula (biology), who was eight months from retirement.

Breasts were a common topic of discussion these days, what with Peg having given birth in May. They were always popping up in one context or another. The bags of breast milk in the staff fridge, for example. Or yesterday during lunch duty, Peg flanked by students in the hallway, fanning miserably at the wet saucers on her shirt with a stack of quizzes, snapping at kids who looked too long, "Problem?"

Peg sat down next to Helen, sighed, and began plucking mushrooms from her packaged salad—which, she reasoned, canceled out the mac and cheese—and hurling them somewhere near the trash can. "Look at you," Peg said. "Peanut butter! So unassuming and almost"—she held a mushroom by her eye like a monocle—"*Puritan!* Maybe if I ate like you I could get rid of these fucking hams." She jiggled her arms as if shaking maracas.

There was something gloriously self-deprecating about Peg. She'd share anything. The evolution of her breasts ("Prego tits—*fabulous!* Post-prego tits—*fucking disturbing!*"). The way her husband's penis could move in figure eights ("I mean, it should be in one of those caves at the bottom of the Atlantic!"). The brutal, criminal agony of eleven ("Eleven!") days without shitting so much as a pebble. Peg lived her life without apology: the Odyssean affair with her husband while he was still married to someone else; sex by email; eloping with him, finally, two hours after the divorce came through, in a rowboat on the Lamprey River with her favorite potted plant aboard. And now she was happier than Helen had ever seen her, with a baby and big, leaky, romantic breasts.

That night Helen sat on the couch in front of the TV with her husband, Tim, a cookie sheet of nachos spanning their knees like a tabletop, a big dumpling of cheese congestion in her throat, a second glass of red wine in her hand, the cat, Doris, shredding the armchair, and the two of them, agreeably buzzed, laughing at her like proud parents.

She hadn't mentioned the Becky Fairchild dilemma to Tim. She wasn't going to grade essays either, because Tim had illegally downloaded a Cary Grant movie for her—risking imprisonment, now *that* was romantic! He didn't like Cary Grant, but was sighing contentedly just the same, pennies of dried ice cream on his shirt. Tim often wore the same clothes for days in a row. He didn't see this as an issue of hygiene so much as one of masculinity—a real man, he joked, didn't care about a clean shirt. Easygoing, that's what everyone said about him, and it was true. Just last week his fingers had swelled mysteriously to zucchinis—he was allergic to everything, poor bastard—and he'd just had a good laugh when he couldn't zip his pants. The guy took everything in stride. He'd even been in his crappy assistant manager position at GameStop for six years, taking constant abuse from that pasty-faced prick with the bad gums, Randy, without so much as asking for a raise.

What a trouper.

Though asking for a raise wouldn't have been the worst thing.

Nor would looking for an actual job with a salary.

It was possible, Helen thought, as she staggered downstairs naked on a nightly basis to stare at the bank balance and scribble figures on a napkin like something out of *The Shining*, that one could take things a little too much in stride. Upstairs, Tim would be peacefully drooling into his own ear, and when she finally slumped back to bed, shivering, he'd curl around her and go *pat, pat* on her hip.

But it was hard for Tim—for anyone!—to find a decent job

without a degree, and not everyone was suited for college. Not having a degree didn't mean Tim wasn't smart. There were all kinds of smart. He had just installed the new windows by himself, more or less without incident, and he'd rearranged all the electronics cords so they were connected to one giant power strip. Now he was building their new computer from scratch, its shiny, angular organs arriving daily by mail and accumulating on the dining room table. She liked that he had talents she did not.

After the movie was over, Tim turned on the baseball game, and Helen drew a bath, lit candles, and killed the lights.

Twenty minutes later Tim came clomping into the bathroom.

"How's the bath?" he asked, lifting the toilet seat.

"Super nice," she said, her ass squeaking on the porcelain. *Super nice?* Wrong tone, kind of Barbie, but what the hell. Maybe he'd grab a washcloth, lower himself to his knees, and coax his hand between her legs, all with a healthy amount of sloshing around. Or just pull her out like a mermaid and take her right there on the bathroom floor. At least her tits weren't sore like Peg's from all that nursing—which, when you thought about it, seemed a little gross.

But no. Tim took a piss, scrutinized his receding hairline in the mirror, and brushed his teeth.

"Great game," Tim said, mouth full of froth. "You should have seen this catch, Damon dove, literally *dove*"—he demonstrated with outstretched hands, toothpaste plopping to the floor—"to catch it."

Peg's husband rubbed her breasts with St. John's wort oil every night. According to Peg, it was positively rapturous.

Every night! St. John's wort!

Whatever that was.

But every couple had different time lines. Peg had gotten pregnant in the first place only because he was twenty years older, and unless she wanted him clip-clopping his walker to their kid's sixth-grade graduation, she said, it was time to get cracking.

"So," Ron Meriwether, headmaster, began the next morning. "You come to me with a problem." There was a good chance he was attempting his Don Corleone impression, which was known to emerge on Fridays and was agreed among the staff best to ignore.

"It's come to my attention," she said, "that Becky Fairchild plagiarized an essay for my class."

Ron tucked both hands under his armpits and kicked his slippers onto his desk—Pajama Day. This week was really getting brutal. Ron was even wearing a nightcap like something out of *A Christmas Carol*.

"Becky Fairchild," he said.

Helen couldn't help noticing that his stomach was really letting loose in those flannel pants. What did the kids call it? A FUPA? Kind of funny, really, almost sounded like it looked, like a visual onomatopoeia, or was there a term for that, when something—

"Becky is applying early decision to Stanford," Ron said.

"She mentioned that. But anyone can *apply* to Stanford. Big Bird could probably—"

"The Fairchilds plan for her to go there."

"At any rate," she said. "It's such a strange choice of essay. So obscure, really. I wonder how she even—"

"The *Fairchilds* Fairchilds."

Helen stared at him.

"As in, Fairchild Hall, Fairchild Auditorium."

"That must be nice for them," she said.

"Helen, Helen," he said. He was standing up now and gazing at his *Blues Brothers* poster. "This is some heavy stuff you're dropping in my lap. And this week of all weeks. I think we should calm down and get our priorities straight. Think big picture." He eyed her outfit, another combination of gray things with cat hair on them. "Where's your pj's?" he said. "Where's your spirit?"

"If you're busy with these festivities I can just go ahead and call—"

"I'm telling you to leave it alone, Helen."

Ron reached under his desk and pulled out the oversized head of the school's mascot, a black bear. He grinned, ripped off his sleeping cap, and put the headpiece on. "Duty calls!" he said, his voice muffled as if he were a plumber under the sink, and he gave Helen two thumbs up as he left.

Ron had never read *Jane Eyre*. Helen would put money on it.

Helen poked her head into Peg's class and motioned for her to come into the hall. As a nod to Pajama Day, Peg wore a sleep mask pushed up like sunglasses on her head. "No," she said, after Helen told her about Becky. "Nope, no. Wrong battle."

Peg kept checking on her students through the door crack, as if peeking in on a baby in a nursery. Her room was dark and smelled woodsy from the candle she kept burning in violation of the fire code. She had a few throw rugs scattered around and a dim lamp with a bamboo shade on her desk. Everyone was working quietly. The low lighting seemed to have a calming effect on the kids, like a blanket over a birdcage. Helen's class, on the other hand, felt like a hospital waiting room: fluorescents glaring, everyone bloodshot and edgy and expecting the worst.

"I'll just call and tell them," Helen said.

"And say what? It won't go anywhere."

"It's the principle."

"The principle is they give like a million a year."

"Yeah, and their kid's a cheater."

"Oh my God," Peg said. "A rich kid's a cheater."

"Tell me you get it."

"Of course I get it. But Ron's just trying to keep your job."

Helen was quiet.

"Pull your head out of your ass. Make her write an extra paper." She gave Helen a colluding nudge. "Lighten up. Have an orgasm." The bell rang. Peg touched her breasts and winced. "I'll find you at the clown fest later," she said. "If anyone needs me for the next fifteen, I'll be pumping in my car like a pervert."

* * *

It wasn't that Helen hadn't had an orgasm. She had! Once, her teeth had even tingled as if she'd bitten down on aluminum foil. That afterglow had lingered for hours, a low-level hum, like sand stirred from the bottom of a river after a heavy landing of, say, a dumped body—well, *that* wasn't sexy, Christ, but maybe something else heavy like—Well, it wasn't so much *what* was landing that was the point, but—

Or maybe it was more like the deliciousness of scratching an itch, say, in the middle of a body cast, near the navel or inner thigh, only reachable by the precise and patient searching of a very long wooden stick. Of course she understood the musical equivalent, too: crescendo, diminuendo. And *climax*, the word itself so literary. Yes, she could come with the best of them, and would again soon (no one could possibly go this long), and maybe at lunch she could volunteer a tidbit between bites of PB and J, a casual reference to having sex on the dryer, or the way Tim's dick did circus—

Everything had been so exciting at first: the frenzied but purposeful lovemaking, the breathy promises, the rhapsodic late hours spent imagining the collision of egg and sperm, which appeared in Helen's mind like an abstract painting.

But lately tact was at a premium: Tim's abstracted pounding, the cat joyfully licking her own ass at the head of the bed, Helen riffling through her repertoire of fantasies, trying each one out for a few seconds before stumbling to the next, flustered and panicky, like a contestant in some terrible game show: *What Scenario Will Bring Home the Big O?* Will it be (A) stranded, need ride, must strip, etc. for rude Mack truck driver.

Or (B) stranded, need ride, must strip, etc. for two rude Mack truck drivers. Or—

When you got down to it, Helen wasn't feeling all that great about herself. All her underpants, for instance, were so stretched out she could practically tuck her tits into them—and hers were tiny, i.e., high up, so she was talking a real problem here—pairs and pairs of these baggy things kept appearing—voila!—as if planted by some asshole fairy. Like, what the hell. And no, okay, all right, she hadn't gotten new ones yet. Because, you know, she had so much goddamn *free time* to shop. Because, no problem, she could just leave her work at work, like Tim at GameStop. A few times the grading had gotten so bad that she'd thrown a whole stack of papers in the trash and told the kids she'd left them on a plane. Not that she'd been on a plane lately.

"Just give them all As!" Tim said now, beer in hand, picking up an essay from the kitchen table where Helen was grading and reading from it in a British accent. He was always speaking in different personas: Yoga Teacher, Distressed Pilot, Hairdresser from Milan. He had designated voices for the cat, who had a lisp, and the houseplants, which were all apparently from Soviet Russia, and, depending on his level of alcohol consumption, his penis. It was like living on a late-night Muppet set.

"Hey, Tim?" she'd whispered the other night, pointing at his crotch with her pen. "Maybe you could ask your pal there to find you a job."

"You're both young," the gynecologist had said to them on

Monday, smoothing his chipper yellow tie. "Try to reconnect. There is always more going on there than you think."

Helen nodded. Tim helped himself to a mint from the hospitable bowl on the doctor's desk. Everyone shook hands.

The guy had a point, Tim suggested on the way home. They could cool it on the baby thing. They were only thirty-two. Did they really want to end up like their friends, who barely recognized their own lives, carting diaper bags and breast pumps, serving chocolate milk to grubby playdates, sitting down to a life of bottomless worry?

It was something to think about.

Friday's last block was replaced by the school's pep rally, the climax of Spirit Week, an overstimulating affair for which Helen forgot every year to call out sick. Teachers with fourth block free were lucky enough to sneak off to their sunbaked Hondas, which would take them even farther, to their homes or a peacefully abandoned beach, or better yet to Rocko's, where pints were two bucks before five o'clock. But Helen had to chaperone for the hour and a half of sensory vandalism.

Only half-full, the gymnasium was already crowded and ripe. Beads of sweat caught the floodlights like sequins. Three rows down, Kyle Parker squirted an angry nest of silly string into Maggie Beaudoin's ballet bun. Trevor Bass was sitting quietly and rocking, a penis-and-balls configuration painted on his cheek. Hopefully someone else would deal with that. Helen didn't feel like breaking the news to him that he had a pink dick on his face. She wasn't sure how many friends he had to begin with—a few Dungeons & Dragons types at best. And with that strange rocking, she could only imagine what kind of show he went home to every evening.

Helen had a stack of *Jane Eyre* essays on her lap. She eyed the doors and imagined darting for the parking lot, the essays scattering behind her. Her students were already so bored and cynical, and she kept losing control of the conversation—like this morning, when Amy Erikkson asked how you had sex with a blind man, anyway, and Keith Havers suggested helpfully that Rochester might have occasionally "taken Jane in the wrong hole." Yes, those papers could just impale themselves on the prickle bushes out front.

Richard Kensington sat down next to her and straightened his pants legs. He hadn't worn pajamas either, but then, he was an odd bird, always frowning when he spoke and carrying around leather-bound Vonnegut like a newborn. She would have thought Richard, who claimed to have read *Lolita* in the fourth grade, would have appreciated Jane's passion, her agony, her quiet resolve. But what had he picked for a topic? Trees. The symbolism of trees.

"How are you finding the pep rally so far, Ms. Fiore?" he said.

"How am I *finding* it?" Richard was really too much. Helen watched Ron on the gym floor, wearing his bear head and teetering in circles, the slippers a special touch, sweat spreading under his arms (What had he told her today? To calm down?), the cheerleaders jumping and clapping frantically every time that asshole—

"I've been wondering," Richard said, his voice dropping to a tone of avuncular concern, "why you never pursued a PhD in literature. I imagine you would have found it rewarding."

Helen nearly choked on her water, just short of spewing it theatrically across his pressed pants. What, did he think teaching high school was not a fulfilling enough career path for someone as capable as her, she, Helen, Ms. Fiore, his AP English teacher? Squandered potential—was that it? A rose without sun?

"I wanted to teach a younger age group," she said.

"Brilliant," he said.

Brilliant? Richard would probably go to Bard and start wearing a beret. Walk around with a fucking ukulele.

"The PhD's value has become diluted," he said. "I've read that more and more students finish their programs with very low chances of job placement."

"Sounds like I dodged a bullet," Helen said. As if she'd enjoyed giving up that spot at Stanford. As if she would have minded wallowing in dissertation angst, fabulously ulcerated from too many cappuccinos, instead of driving her mother to every goddamn bar on the coast and flashing her father's license. *Has he been here tonight?*

"What did you think of *Jane Eyre*?" she asked him.

"Very enjoyable."

"The love story, though. Did you like it?"

Richard brushed a fleck of glitter from his wrist. "Brontë's rendering seemed a touch overwrought."

"Really."

"That was my impression."

"Overwrought."

"I could be wrong."

"Brontë's trees, though, you didn't have a problem with those? The vegetation was properly wrought?"

"Sorry?"

"Got a girlfriend, Richard?" she said.

He began to stand up, straightening those pants again.

"Or boyfriend—whoops!"

He was muttering something about the bathroom.

"Dick, hey," she called to his back, as he cautiously made his way down the bleacher stairs. "We don't have to talk about that!"

Dick? Jesus. There was nothing wrong with ukuleles. Who was she to knock ukuleles? Ukuleles were great. Maybe if she had had a goddamn music lesson or two, she'd know the difference between that and say, a wha'-d'ya-call-it. A banjo. Equally great. She'd praise his tree analysis in class. It was an original idea, after all, with authoritative topic sentences!

Helen scanned the gymnasium for other teachers, to see if anyone else was feeling a bit taxed. There was Carla (earth science), hearing aids strategically MIA, standing up over and over to smooth her skirt under her ass. Larry (American history) leaning against the climbing wall with his eyes closed, likely doing one of those breathing exercises he'd started after his wife ran off with an actual circus clown. Margaret (geography) officiously ripping a megaphone out of some freshman's hands and dropping it on her foot. Helen laughed, and then felt guilty and looked down at her own feet. The realization blossomed slowly. It didn't seem possible, but there they were—oh, God. Brown on the left, black on the right. Jesus. Her shoes. Brown and black. Black and brown. Not even the same shoe. Totally different. One had a buckle and one didn't, for Christ's sake. In the dark of the morning she hadn't noticed. What could she do? Nothing. There was no getting around a thing like that. You either had on two different shoes or you didn't.

And she did.

She could say it was—*it was for Clash Day!*

Perfect. Perfecto.

She felt a lightness, even, at the genius of it. Things really did, after all, work out for the best. All was well in her world, she was whole and complete, just as Louise Hay said. Perhaps people had been admiring her! Maybe she had even scored herself some cred, like: *Hey, that Ms. Fiore, she's some hot—*

No.

Fuck her. No Clash. *Yesterday was Clash.*

Today was—

She looked around. Pajama Day.

Well, shoes weren't pajamas. Shoes were duds. Shoes were the Scrooge of Pajama Day. Who went to bed in shoes? No one. No one except Dad. Dad had. But that wasn't the same. That hadn't been really *going* to bed, but more like being unconscious in a horizontal position.

She could just take them off and shove them in her school

bag, walk around in socks, boom. All cool, casual, like, yeah, no big deal. Bingo. All part of the plan, whichever way you cut it. Why not? School spirit. She would. She did.

Her left toe stuck tragically through a hole in her sock.

Helen stared. There was nothing worse than that. There were few things worse than that. Like those nipple hairs she had started tweezing while she brushed her teeth. One day she probably wouldn't even bother, and then she'd be eighty, and then she'd be dead and she would never have felt—*what?* No, she would, she would, for Christ's sake, no one lived an entire whole life without—

Peg was sitting a few rows in front of Helen, with her cowboy boots, and flattering layers to hide her beautiful baby weight, and that sleep mask—so perfect, really. Why hadn't Helen thought of that? Why couldn't Helen just go with the flow like that? There she was, laughing in a gracious way at Ron, whose bear head was now resting on his flanneled lap like a pet. He appeared to be performing a comedic act with flamboyant hand gestures and busy eyebrows. Peg was enjoying herself as usual, unfazed by her proximity to the loudspeakers and Ron's breath.

The athletics director, John Turner, was at the podium, rattling off this season's stats like something from the stock exchange: "Field hockey, three and oh, soccer, two and four . . ." Helen imagined walking up to the podium, pushing eight-foot John aside: *Hello, hi, people, what a pep rally, yes yes, anyone remember how Jane knows to return to Rochester? Anyone? Fucking telepathy! Now* that's *a soul mate! Woo-hoo! Let's give it up for Jane and—*

Maybe she had ADHD or—

After such a god-awful childhood, to finally find a home with the one you loved more than—to need to be with some-one that much—to *know* that one man was your soul's other—

"Helen!"

Someone was calling her name.

"Helen! Helen!"

Well, it sure as hell wasn't Tim, who barely called her from the other side of the couch, let alone from across a hundred miles of heather or peat moss or whatever.

"I am coming!" Helen cried out into the crowd. "Wait for me! Oh, I will come!" Jesus, she was really starting to lose—

"You okay?" It was Peg, who was now sitting beside Helen, patting her knee. "Why are you yelling?"

"It's just part of a book." Helen groaned into her hands. "It's just been a long day, you know? Sometimes you just . . ."

Peg touched Helen's arm, and Helen suddenly felt very far away. She wanted to crawl under the bleachers in that dim cor-ner with the fire extinguisher and the stack of purple exercise mats. That wouldn't be an issue, would it, just a few minutes in the fetal position?

"You should go home." Peg snatched the pile of *Jane Eyre* essays from Helen's lap and began straightening it. "You look weird. I've been watching you from over there."

"I'm fine. I was going to read the rest of these."

"I'll watch your students."

"Relax, I'm perfectly—"

"It's Friday," Peg said. "You guys have plans?"

Becky Fairchild was at the podium, wrapped in the arms

of Tammy, the field hockey coach, gripping a plaque of some sort against her chest.

"Plans?" Helen said. "I don't know."

Helen didn't catch what the award was for, but everyone seemed pretty happy about it. Best plagiarizer?

"Make some!" Peg said. "What about a picnic? God, that sounds nice. A fall picnic. Wine and cheese, a crunchy baguette. I'm really into fig . . ."

The crowd began to holler. Becky shook her plaque in the air. What was Becky wearing? Helen squinted.

". . . or jump in the car and drive to Provincetown. Find a bed-and-breakfast. Quick, before you get knocked up and never . . ."

A Stanford T-shirt.

"Shit," Peg was saying. "I'd give my left labia to get a weekend alone with Marc."

"'No woman was ever nearer to her mate than I am,'" Helen said.

"Huh?"

"'Ever more absolutely bone of his bone and flesh of his flesh.'"

"Who, Tim?" Peg said.

"*Tim?*"

Fine, she'd leave. The stupid day was practically over, anyway. She stood up. She was going. She was shoving right past everyone to the bleacher stairs. Down the stairs. Black, brown. It wasn't an issue. Right past poor rocking Trevor with his porno paint job, right past Ron in his pj's FUPA, even, who was waving at her. Ron wasn't bad. Ron was whatever. Ron was what he was. She waved back, was now flashing him a friendly thumbs-up. She would stop for a beer at Rocko's. What the hell. Maybe Tim could meet her there, like in the old days! A little spontaneity. She couldn't remember the last time they'd gone on a date.

Maybe that was all they needed.

Yes.

Out in the hall, she called him on her cell phone. She could get some sharp lipstick at CVS on the way over there, and even a new shirt! She wouldn't get the shirt at CVS, obviously, but maybe—

"Crap," Tim said, after she told him her plan. "I was going to grab a drink with Dan and Neal."

"Oh."

"Tomorrow?"

The animal bellow of an air horn sounded in the gymnasium, and people cheered. She leaned against the cold tiles of the wall and pressed her cheek to them. She closed her eyes, then hung up. Her heart was thumping like a flat tire. What did Jane say? *My heart beat fast and thick: I heard its throb. Suddenly it stood still to an inexpressible feeling that thrilled—*

Helen hadn't had enough lunch; that was all. Another goddamn Puritan peanut butter sandwich. Who'd be satisfied with that? Sometimes her heart flopped around like that when her blood sugar got too—

I know no weariness of my Edward's society: he knows none of mine, any more than we each do of the pulsation of the heart that beats in our separate bosoms; consequently, we are ever togeth—

It was one thing to not get it. Lots of kids didn't get it. But to not even read the fucking thing. To sit there and braid her hair in the back while Helen read passages with such feeling she broke a sweat. All Helen wanted was to share her favorite book, her desert island book, a love story so . . . the kind of love you didn't always . . . the kind of love you might never—

Never find.

Becky couldn't have given less of a shit.

And then to cheat like that.

Helen was pushing the stairwell door open, climbing to the third floor. She was at the top now, walking down the English department hallway. Her door was on the right and she was opening it, closing it behind her without turning on the lights. She was standing at her desk now, flipping through her student rolodex, dialing 9 to make a call. Out the window her favorite maple was already naked, its leaves a red dress around its ankles. She would miss that tree. She would miss that tree a lot. Maybe she would leave a note for her replacement and suggest they take the class under it to read to them from *Winnie-the-Pooh*. The students loved that. You had to do it in the first week of October, between 12:05 and 12:20, when the sun lit the leaves just—

"Mr. Fairchild?" Helen said when a man answered. "Mr. Fairchild, this is Helen Fiore, Becky's AP English teacher."

THE DEVIL'S TRIANGLE

Her parents always said they'd dig their own graves if anything happened to their children, so when her sister Claire disappeared on a camping trip in the White Mountains, Elsie kept
an eye on things. She brought them groceries. Made mushroom risottos and bean enchiladas and coconut lentil soups
and made her father sit at the table until he ate three bites.
Took her mother to cafés downtown to drink cappuccino and
play honeymoon whist. Signed her father up for beach yoga
and dragged him to the ocean at sunrise with bamboo mats.
Researched psychotherapy and cognitive behavioral therapy
and expressive therapy and grief therapy and called psychologists and psychiatrists and support groups and chauffeured
her mother to initial consultations. "I don't need some Welles-
ley cunt taking notes while I play in a sandbox," her mother
would say, sinking into Elsie's Volkswagen, knuckles rough as
burlap and clenching her purse, and Elsie would drive home
and call someone else.

It had been a year of that. Still they knew nothing, and Elsie lived in that nothing, roaming the endless corridors of it, the silence unspeakable and huge.

"Come down for the weekend," Elsie's other sister, Mika, said on the phone. The sisters were triplets. They were twenty-nine. They'd all been sharing an apartment in Cambridge, and when Claire went missing, Mika dropped out of law school and drove south without so much as a map. Before, she had been ambitious and idealistic and high-strung, had volunteered at a women's shelter every night after class got out, had railed daily against the patriarchal machine, had even lasted forty-nine weeks, as far as she knew, without buying a single item made in China. Now she was a secretary at a hearing center and spent all day yelling into the phone at "all the old fucks." Sometimes she didn't answer Elsie's calls for weeks, and when she did, she sounded like someone else, her voice thin and hoarse.

"I don't know," Elsie said.

"Don't you have Columbus Day off?"

Elsie was a high school librarian, a little intense these days, maybe, a little aggressive—*Read this!* she'd say, pushing hardcovers into the chests of bagel-faced linebackers, gloomy and skittish bulimics, gamers with Red Bull teeth. *Just read this!*

"There's shit I have to order," Elsie said.

"Mitchell's having a party on his yacht," Mika said. "You could use a little extroversion. You can practice your small talk."

"Who's Mitchell?" Elsie said.

"My boyfriend."

"I thought François was your boyfriend."

"Who?" Mika said. "Oh, Jacques. Yeah, he was."

"Oh."

"You don't have to say *oh* like that."

"I didn't!" Steam banged, pitchless, up the pipes in the apartment where Elsie still lived. Fall was here, and she hated it—the quick animal scratch of yard rakes, chestnuts dropping like bullets on the tops of cars, the occasional jack-o'-lantern snatched in the night and found murdered in the road. It would snow soon, and nights were getting very dark.

"A *yacht*?" Elsie said.

"A superyacht." Mika sighed. "How long can you do this?"

Elsie looked into Claire's room—surfboard propped against the closet door, cross-country skis tucked under the bed, Buddha statue in the window, boxes of books on large animal husbandry and small animal surgery and fundamental veterinary clinical pathology, harp zipped in its cover, eighteen Japanese teapots Claire had individually named. Mika had sublet her own room to a surgical intern who was never home, but Elsie was still paying for Claire's—she didn't know what else to do. What else could she do? Claire had just run to the bathroom—*Be right back!*—a tampon like a flare in her fist.

"It's just for the time being," Elsie said.

"Use my miles."

Elsie knocked on Mika's door, woozy from the flight, taxi backing up and bobbing over a succession of speed bumps.

Cadillacs and Buicks sat in assigned covered parking spots. Anoles darted out from bushes and scaled the concrete stairs. Gnomes pushed gnome wheelbarrows in rock gardens. Mika didn't have a garden, just a piece of trellis that didn't quite hide the gas tank. After returning from a cross-country road trip, Claire had once proclaimed that Florida—blue hairs vying for discounted cinnamon buns, alligators loitering in soupy meridians, palm trees nothing but poles with bad hats—on her personal Spectrum of Existential Angst (SEA, she called it, for short), was an eleven. But here Mika had landed, in a condo complex on the yellowed outskirts of Miami.

Mika opened the door with a whoosh of central air, beer in hand. "I got out of work early," she said, squeezing Elsie hard. "Said I had diarrhea." She did not look well. Her hair was blond now, and it didn't suit her. Her skin and lips looked washed out, the pouches under her eyes dark as figs.

"Are you eating?" Elsie said.

"Yes, I'm *eating*." She took Elsie's bag and dropped it in the front hall. "Bathroom's that way."

Elsie walked around Mika's condo. A TV the size of a milk truck shouted local news. She studied framed pictures of people she had never seen, grinning wildly with their faces pushed together, colored drinks raised to the camera, doing Jell-O shots, belly shots. It took Elsie a few seconds to recognize her sister in them at all. Elsie wandered into the small lanai and looked at the fountain in the center of a man-made pond.

"Water view, baby," Mika said, when Elsie walked back in.

"Very nice," Elsie said, and Mika handed her a Corona.

Under the overhead light, Mika's skin looked green as a grass stain. Claire had always tended to the lighting in the girls' apartments, swapping 100 watts out for 60 watts, making sure they felt cozy and at ease. She would turn on a lamp, walk to the other end of the room, and grimace. *What do you think?* she'd say to Elsie or Mika, who would nod, shrug, but Claire would already be stomping toward it, ripping off the shade, wringing the lamp by the neck. *Depressing,* she'd say. *Looks like the kind of hotel room you die in.*

"Go sit in the sun," Mika said. "I'll bring out some lunch."

Elsie walked onto the small backyard. A few hibiscuses bloomed, blossoms as big as cats. The yard had a stone patio, a glass table with an umbrella, and a gas grill tucked in the corner by an animal cage and two recycling bins so full of liquor bottles that several empty handles had been placed on the ground. She walked over and crouched to look inside the mesh hut. Claire's guinea pig, Pam, sat on chicken wire, breathing rapidly. Mika had taken her when she moved out of the apartment. Now the animal was barely recognizable, polka-dotted with scarlet sores like sucked cough drops, her nails brown and corkscrewing into her feet, her left eye oozed shut, the right cloudy as if rinsed with half-and-half.

Elsie reached into the cage to pet her.

Mika emerged from the condo carrying two sandwiches on plates. "Courtesy of Miracle Hearing," she said. When the doctors had lunch meetings, she could, if timed right, score a leftover sandwich. If you threw those things in the toaster oven, she said, boom: dinner. "I added mustard."

"Looks like Pam's been doing some hard living," Elsie said.

Mika shrugged and handed Elsie a plate. "She's happy."

"Happy?" Elsie eyed the sandwich warily.

"Well, I don't know! You can't tell with those things." Mika bent over and stared blankly into the cage. "They don't bring much to the table."

"Jesus," Elsie said. "You have to feed her."

Mika dropped into a chair and began to eat. "I feed her," she said with her mouth full, "and at six we have cocktails."

"I'm serious. Claire will frea—"

"Okay, boss," Mika said. She set her plate on the arm of the chair, pulled a pack of cigarettes from her pocket, and shook one out.

"You smoke?" Elsie said. The sandwich was stale as a paperback.

"Not really."

"Don't do that. I'm begging you."

"You got bigger problems," Mika said, cupping her hand over the lighter. She blew a woolly stream from the side of her mouth. "You should see your eye right now. *Wandering*'s a word for it."

"Yeah, well," Elsie said. Pam hadn't moved. A nauseous breeze drifted over from the cage. "It's been doing that lately."

Mika cringed. "That's fucked," she said.

"What's Mitchell like?" Elsie said, after they'd finished eating and Mika suggested they go for a walk. "Besides owning a yacht." The road was a three-lane highway, and not, Elsie was realizing, on the way to something else. This, the highway, was the walk. Storm clouds billowed from a Mack. An old Pontiac dragged its muffler like a car of newlyweds.

"He's—" Mika frowned. "He has this space between his front teeth. And when he smiles his eyes get all squinty. He likes to fuck me in front of the window. Says it's not fair he's the only one who gets to see me."

Elsie made a face. "How charitable."

Mika was pumping her arms, her hands in fists. "I think he's great," she said.

Elsie shrugged. "Is it serious?"

"Ehh," Mika said. "He does his own thing."

"So you just stay in touch?"

"He might text, like, twice a week?"

"Do you text him?" Elsie said.

"Well, I *respond*," Mika said. "You can't seem too needy or they'll lose interest."

A woman stood on her deck, stomach hanging out, clutching a beer and looking out over the traffic, and Elsie waved. "That's needy?" she said.

"He likes to come and go."

"And you're okay with that."

"What?"

"I don't know," Elsie said. "Really, what do I know?" Mika had always insisted that dating culture was yet another mass conspiracy—along with toothpaste, manholes, airline snacks—of female subjugation. Once, when Elsie had been considering quitting her job to be near an old boyfriend, Mika asked her if she needed a fucking ambulance, and then didn't talk to her for a month.

Those beers had been a bad move. Mika, who'd had six, maybe seven, didn't seem fazed. Elsie took off her long-sleeved shirt and wiped down her chest with it. Men leaned out of a roofless Jeep, hooting.

"When are you going back to school?" Elsie said.

"I'm not."

"I don't understand."

Mika shrugged. "I didn't really want to be a lawyer."

At the grounds, after two hours had passed, having checked every bathroom, parking lot, and campsite, Elsie and Mika had stumbled blind into separate parts of the woods, their calls like echoes of each other. *Claire! Claire!*

"Right," Elsie said. "You wanted to be a secretary."

They came to a rest stop near a city reservoir, and Mika pointed to a bench next to some porta-potties. "This is my favorite spot," she said. "Let's sit, okay? Let's just sit for a minute."

They sat.

Construction trucks howled behind them. The porta-potties smelled syrupy and rank. A diesel breeze shuffled her bangs. "Did you have to put her out by the trash?" Elsie said finally.

"What are you talking about?"

"Pam."

Mika sighed. "You saw my yard. It's a fucking bathroom mat. Everything's technically *by the trash*."

Elsie watched her suck on a cigarette, and then she looked away, out at the gunmetal water, at the wires strung from pole to pole to ward off the birds.

There was a pair of Frye boots Mika needed at Nordstrom. "When you divide the price by every day I'll wear them," she said, "they're practically free." Then she wanted to go to Victoria's Secret.

Mitchell, she said, preferred her in the push-up.

"Who *are* you?" Elsie said, eyes wide.

"What do you mean?"

"I don't know," Elsie said. "Nothing." She could smell the store's perfume from the street. Naked, decapitated mannequins stood in the window.

"Let's get you something sexy," Mika said. "My treat."

"What happened to your whole theory on the conspiracy of commercialized objectification?" Elsie said. "Or whatever you called it."

"We'll give them dirty looks," Mika said, pulling Elsie by the elbow into the store.

There was the kind that showed a quarter of your ass. There was the kind that showed half of your ass. Then there was the rest. Striped, hearted, leopard. Bows and buckles. Stores like this always made Elsie feel like an impostor. You either had sex appeal, she thought, or you didn't, like attached earlobes. Claire had it. It was something about the way she walked, Elsie thought. She took her time. She used her hips. She didn't scurry out of the room like a shoplifter.

"Try these," Mika said, pointing to a table. "And these."

Elsie scanned Mika's face for a hint of cynicism, of irony, but she was flipping assertively through a pile of "cheekies" fanned out like a platter of cold cuts.

"You know those cotton ones that Claire wears?" Elsie said. "Are those here? I'd wear those."

Mika was tearing through a hanger of bras. "Hmm," she said.

Elsie thumbed the material. "Do you think Victoria's secret is that she has a yeast infection?" she said.

Mika's phone began to ring.

"Your phone," Elsie said.

"I've got it," Mika said, reaching for her bag.

"It's in your purse."

"Obviously."

Mika had found Claire's flip-flop a hundred feet from the bathrooms. *It's hers!* she'd yelled, beginning to sob, her face scratched red, from a branch or her own fingernails. *It's Claire's!*

Elsie stared at Mika, clutching a pair of underwear in her fist. "Who is it?" she said.

"Hold *on*," Mika said. She squinted at the phone, then shook her head and dropped it back into her purse.

"Tell me," Elsie said.

"Eight hundred number."

"Oh."

They went back to the underwear.

"Is this what you'd call 'taking back our sexuality'?" Elsie said. Her pulse was throwing punches. She held up a black G-string. "Do you think this thong is third-wave or post-feminist?"

"Just pick out a few fucking panties."

"I'll get this." Elsie swung the thong. "It can double as an eye patch."

"Seriously," Mika said.

"I am serious."

"Pick something out for real."

Elsie dutifully flipped through a rack of polyester teddies. She tried hard to have an opinion about them, or else not to have an opinion about them—she wasn't sure which. She supposed they were nice, the teddies. She supposed she could use one. She held one up and studied it.

"Do you have any in an A cup?" Elsie asked one of the salesgirls.

"A cups are only sold online."

"What are you saying?" Elsie said hotly, and then shuffled apologetically behind a mannequin.

Mika came out of the dressing room. "Did you see these dresses over here?" she said. "I could see you in one of these." They were black, silky, with thin straps. Mika grabbed one and handed it to her sister. Elsie held it against her torso and looked down dubiously.

"My bush'll fall out," she said.

"Good. You're wearing it tonight. Phil will be into it."

"Phil?"

"That guy I told you about."

"No, you didn't."

"Oh," Mika said. "He's a friend of Mitch's. I told him you were coming."

"I'm not in the mood for that."

Mika's eyes grew wet, veiny as leaves, and she looked away.

"I'd prefer to be clothed," Elsie said.

Mika bought the dress for Elsie and five new bras for herself. They walked out into the afternoon sun. Palm leaves clattered like bones above them. "Now let's get your hair done," said Mika.

"I just got it cut."

"Highlights. Just a few."

"Mika."

Elsie's hair, two hours later, was a parched blond, coarse and stringy as a doll's.

"You look like a different person!" Mika said, clapping, when the foil came off.

"Like you?" Elsie snapped, and then excused herself to the bathroom and sat on the floor. The plunger next to her had been recently used. She looked at it for a while, at the slick pottery glaze of it, and then retched into the toilet.

Mika was helping Mitchell set up for the party and had left cab fare and the address of the marina for Elsie while she took a nap and then a shower. She was to be there at five, Mika said, no later. It was already twenty past. The dress was light as a kerchief when Elsie took it out of the bag. She put it on—thong, too—and walked around the empty condo, her wet hair dripping down her shoulders, her legs, already ugly with winter, jutting out from the dress. It seemed impossible that the day was not yet over. It seemed more than impossible that there was a party tonight and she would be at it. She realized she didn't have any shoes, so she put her sneakers back on and then looked in the mirror. Her hair didn't seem attached to her at all but positioned on top of her, stiffly, like wicker.

She called a cab, and then went outside to see if Pam had eaten any of the lettuce she had put in the cage. It hadn't been touched. She nudged a leaf under Pam's chin, and then tapped the water bottle to let a few drips out.

"Hold on," whispered Elsie. "Please."

She stood there for a minute, while the one cloud in Florida sat on the sun, which made all the birds sing out, in bursts, like music boxes opened and slammed shut again.

Then she pulled Pam out, and when the cab came, she buckled herself in and Pam, too, while she was at it.

At the marina in South Beach, the sun was dropping to the sea, lighting up sails like Chinese lanterns. Elsie padded along the boardwalk, gripping Pam to her chest. Three sheepish-looking pelicans hung their heads on the dock. A group of women approached her, and they parted down the middle for Elsie. For a moment she was swallowed in shampoo and chatter and cigarettes, and then she emerged from the other side and kept walking. Her hair rustled in the wind.

Narrow-eyed yachts glowed like a neighborhood: *Knot His*, *Atta Buoy*, *Alimony*. Elsie wasn't big on parties. She wasn't big on boats either. Blinking Christmas lights were strung along the railing. A server, a little too tan, greeted her as she stepped on board. So this was a superyacht. "Veuve Clicquot?" he asked. His teeth were as white as his gloves. She tugged her dress downward. "No, thank you," she said.

"Christ, finally!" Mika said, clomping down from the upper deck, gin and tonic in hand. The backline of her dress plunged to her tailbone. Her eyeliner extended past her lids and onto her crow's feet, which, now that Elsie thought about it, she had never seen on Mika before, although now her skin was so grooved it seemed she had never been without them.

Mika's eyes darted back and forth from Pam in Elsie's arms, to her sneakers, to her hair, which was still wet and had left water stains above her breasts. Mika sipped her drink. "I see you brought a plus one," she said finally.

"I couldn't leave her out there alone."

"Are you fucking kidding me?" Mika said. "There are some big fucking people here."

"What's with the eyeliner? You trying out for *Cats*?"

Mika grew red in the face. "All day," she said, holding her pointer finger and thumb close together by her face, "you have made me feel this small."

"Mika, look at her."

"She's a guinea pig!" Mika yelled, flinging her arms out by her side. Gin sloshed down her wrist. Her collarbones were bold as handlebars. "She's old. She was old when I took her."

"She didn't have bullet holes when you took her."

"At least I took her."

"Ho, right," Elsie said. "Thanks for all the fucking help."

Pam stank. A woman in crutches swung toward them, grimacing good-naturedly. Her cast disappeared under her dress. "Excuse me," she said, and Elsie smiled and moved out of the way.

"Give me the guinea pig," Mika said. The yacht rumbled and began to pull out of its slip. Gauzy exhaust passed over them.

"What are you *doing* down here?" said Elsie. "I know you hate it. Tell me you hate it."

"Give it to me."

Elsie handed over Pam. She followed Mika down the corridor into a small storeroom, where Mika put her into an empty liquor carton and then tucked the box under a leather bench.

"Mika, please," Elsie said. "Why are we here?" She reached her hand out, but her sister swatted it away.

"When's your flight?" Mika said.

"Sunday."

"Change it to tomorrow," Mika said, and then she disappeared down the corridor and up the stairs.

When Elsie finally wandered to the upper deck, tearful and trembling, there were about three dozen people milling around holding oily napkins of spinach triangles and coconut shrimp stuck with toothpicks. There was a long table with a white cloth and silver serving platters of food. There was a bartender standing behind a small city of liquor bottles. There was a pool.

Elsie fixed herself a plate and made her way to the far corner of the deck by the deep end. The craft approached a jetty.
Vietnamese women sat on rocks, crabbing. She waved but they
didn't see her. She waved again, but they didn't see her that
time either, and she turned her attention to her food, pushing
blood clots of tomato sauce around with her fork. The eggplant
was tough, greasy as eel, and she ate it quickly, the urge to cry
hot in her throat. She scanned the deck for Mika, but she didn't
see her anywhere.

"Elsie?" someone said.

"Hmm-hmm!" Elsie swallowed without chewing and
turned around to see a man, muscular, lumpy, and packed as
a yam display, in a Hawaiian shirt at least three sizes too small.

"Phil," he said, extending his hand. "Mika said I should
find you." He smiled at her feet. "New Balance?"

Elsie looked down. "Had an emergency," she said.

"Your heel break?"

"No, I—"

"That was always happening to my wife. She'd be walking
along and then, *snap!*"

"Heels are awful," she agreed.

He shrugged. "She's fat."

"Oh."

"She's not fat," he said.

"Okay." She sighed anxiously and looked around. Build-
ings were growing farther and farther away, small as teeth.
"Wife?" she said.

"At a certain point you think you have a handle on your

life," he started. "Maybe you're not *happy* happy, you know, but you're not on meds." He sighed. "Then you wake up one day and you realize you've put all your eggs in a lesbian basket." He tried to finish his beer, but there was too much in his glass and it sloshed down the sides of his mouth. "Ah, shit," he said, and started to dab at his shirt.

"Oh, so—" She looked at him, then away, at the runny egg of the sun, then back at him.

"Bingo."

She sipped her drink. "Maybe that's better than her loving another man."

"I don't think so."

"At least you know she didn't leave for a bigger cock," she blurted. "She just left them all on the table, period."

His coloring moved around his face and stuck there, in patches. "All cocks on the table," he said.

"And even if it were smallish," she continued, waving her hand meaningfully in the direction of his pants—*Maybe next time*, Claire had once said after a double date, *focus more on eating*—"that would be a moot point. I mean, I would think the smaller, for her, the more, ah, palatable." Should she leap off this yacht buzzed or plastered? She looked away, embarrassed, looked anywhere, at her tragic sneakers, at the woman across the deck also looking at her sneakers, at pelicans plunging into the water, and settled finally on his arm hair, which was so long it actually swayed a little in the wind, like wheat.

"She hasn't left," he said.

"Oh."

"Not technically."

"I see."

"Her stuff's still at the house. I told her she could keep it there until she figures things out."

"Right."

"Everyone keeps telling me to move on," Phil said miserably. "Just start a new life. But I just can't seem to—" He looked away and then back, staring blankly. "I was hoping she was going through a phase."

She tried to think of something to say. "I like your shirt," she said.

He looked down, making a double chin, and plucked at the material. "I did a wash yesterday and now this seems a little small."

"It's very festive."

"Not that I'm one of those guys who can't do stuff around the house!" he said. "You should see the tub when I'm done with it."

"Be right back, okay?" Elsie said. "I'd love another drink?"

At the food table she grabbed a few cucumber sticks and then hurried down to the lower deck. A couple was kissing in the corridor. The woman made soft whining noises and stepped out of her shoes. "Excuse me," Elsie said, pushing past them. The door to the storeroom was open slightly, and she ducked inside.

She found the bench and knelt down to pull the box out. Pam was there, panting, her fur almost damp to the touch. Elsie didn't know what she'd been thinking. She put the cucumbers down, slumped onto the shrimp-smelling carpet, and tried the deep-breathing exercises she had read about in one of her mother's handouts: inhale for four, hold for four, exhale for eight. She could hear Mika in the corridor. "Mitch, where *are* you?" she was yelling. She sounded drunk. "Mitch, baby, come on!"

"Mika!" Elsie called out, and waited. "Mika, in here!" But the corridor was quiet again.

Elsie sat there for a while with her head against the wall. Then she gently pushed Pam's box under the bench, staggered back to the upper deck, and threw down another G&T.

Phil was still out by the deep end. "I got you a drink," he said, holding up an empty glass, "but then I drank it."

"No problem."

Mika was stumbling toward them, barefoot, wrapped in a beach towel and clutching a martini. Her eyes were red, sore-looking, sooty with mascara.

"Mika Machine!" Phil said.

Mika eyed him coolly.

"Where's Mitch?" he said. "I have his watch."

"Yeah?" Mika scowled. "Chuck it overboard."

"Ah, well," Phil said. He chuckled nervously.

"You okay?" Elsie said.

"Domestic troubles?" Phil said.

"I need a drink," Mika said, although hers was full.

"Mika," Elsie said. Her sister wouldn't look at her. "What's going on?" she said, but Mika was already wandering down the deck.

"Great girl," Phil said. He watched Mika walk away, then turned back to Elsie and studied her. "Need Dramamine?"

"It's not that."

He nodded sympathetically. "Have your period?"

"Jesus," she said, and leaned over the railing. The sea was ruffled, gray as a hubcap.

"Careful," he said. "Don't lean so far."

"I like it," she said quietly. "You ever get that feeling, like you might jump?"

He looked at her, eyes wide. "I can't swim."

"Should you be on a boat?"

"Ennnh," he said. "You live in Miami, too?"

"Boston," Elsie said. At the edge of the pool, Mika unwrapped her towel and then dropped it to the deck to reveal a white bikini.

"Boston!" He looked momentarily despondent, then recovered. "What do you do in Boston? Do you ski-doo?"

"I'm a librarian." Elsie watched Mika step gingerly into the pool. "I mean I was. I mean I still—at a high school."

"I love the sound of the bindings getting swiped over that detector thing," Phil said. "You know, so the alarm doesn't go off."

"The desensitizer," Elsie said. She looked at him. "You do?"

"Yeah," he said. "I like to check out cookbooks."

"You cook?"

"Not really, but I like the pictures. Also Eleanor Roosevelt biographies. And books on UFOs, sightings and myths and stuff. The Loch Ness Monster, I'm into that. The Devil's Triangle."

She was watching Mika swim toward the deep end. "What's that?" she said.

"You know." He drew a triangle in the air. "Weird stuff happens out there. Ever heard of Flight Nineteen?"

"No."

"USS *Cyclops*?"

Elsie shook her head.

"Vanished without a trace," he said moodily, narrowing his eyes.

Mika was struggling to swim with her drink. Her nose kept dipping under the water, and she began to choke.

Phil pointed to the horizon. "We're sailing into the corner of it now."

"Really," Elsie said.

"Now, let's see." Phil pulled his lips to one side like a drape, thinking. "There was the *Spray*, the *Star Tiger*, the *Star Ariel*, Flight Two-oh-one, the *Piper*—"

"What do you do?" she said tensely. She squinted at the dimming sky. "For work."

"Kind of in between jobs at the moment."

"Sure," Elsie said. Her head felt tingly and dense. In the deep end, Mika grabbed a man by the shoulders and then wrapped her legs around his waist.

"Huh," Elsie said. "I didn't picture Mitchell with a ponytail."

Phil frowned at the pool. "That's Greg," he said.

"Greg."

"People call him Dom."

Elsie looked back at Mika, who was whispering in Dom's ear. She laughed drunkenly, then pulled one triangle of her bikini top to the side until her nipple bobbed out of the water. "Go ahead," Elsie heard Mika say, and Dom reached out and pinched it.

"Wowza," Phil said.

"Where the hell's Mitchell?" Elsie snapped. She pictured sinkholes, quicksand, oceans black and swallowing airplanes, closing over whole destroyers like lips.

Phil chuckled. "I think she's moved on."

"You don't know her." She looked at him darkly. "You don't know anything about her."

"True," Phil said. His hand hovered near her, weirdly, as if trying to land, and she froze while he tucked an imaginary piece of hair behind her ear. "So what's that like?" he said.

"What?" Elsie said.

"You know," Phil said. "Being twins."

Dom had pulled off Mika's bathing suit top and was holding it, teasingly, in the air above her head. "Come on," Mika said, laughing.

"*Twins?*" Elsie said. She looked at Phil. Her blood pressure swooned. Sweat burst from her hairline and the backs of her legs. "We're not just—is that what she said?"

Dom grabbed Mika and spun her around, pinning her

arms behind her back. Then he hoisted her so her breasts stuck out of the water. A few men in the pool started to clap.

"I bet you feel each other's feelings and shit," Phil said. He was stroking the back of her neck. "I bet you have ESP."

"I'd like to be alone," Elsie said edgily.

"Me too," Phil said. He began to play with the strap of her dress. "There's a storeroom downstairs we could—"

She smacked his hand.

"Oof," Phil said, shaking his hand out. "Are you Italian?"

"Are you autistic?"

Phil flinched, stepping back. "You sure you're twins?" he said.

"Excuse me?"

"I thought you'd be like her." He stared dejectedly into the pool. "Keep going," the other men called out. Mika's breasts swung on top of the water. "Take her bottoms off!"

"I figured you'd be fun."

Mika's legs shimmered in the underwater lights.

"Fun like what?" Elsie said. The men were swimming closer.

Phil shrugged and pointed into the pool. "Like that."

Dom tossed the bikini top onto the deck and Mika lunged for it. She slipped in his arms, and the martini glass shattered on the edge of the deck.

The wind caught in Elsie's throat like a gag. "Like that?" she said. She saw Claire's sandal held high in Mika's hand. Squad cars. Their mother's mouth opened in a shriek.

"Yeah."

The men were surrounding Mika now. "Come on," Elsie heard them saying. Mika was struggling up the ladder, covering her breasts with one arm. She slipped on the wet deck, caught herself, and then stumbled toward the stairs.

"You think she's having *fun*?" Elsie snapped.

Then she swiped the bikini top from the deck and ran after her sister.

When Elsie got down the stairs, she couldn't find Mika anywhere. She looked in every cabin and corridor. She ran back up the stairs to the top deck. Phil was fishing through a cooler of beers. Dom and the other two men were tossing a Nerf ball in the pool and talking about the Heat. The bartender was organizing empties behind him in a cardboard box. "Mika!" she yelled, but no one looked over. A crowd of women exploded into false laughter. She ran to the edge of the railing and looked blindly out onto the water, looking but afraid to look, and then staggered back down the stairs.

The bottom level was dark, where everyone was dancing. Rap throbbed out of speakers, over the engine. She tripped over a row of abandoned high heels, steadying herself against a column, and then pushed through the clammy, gyrating crowd. The yacht cut through the sea. She squinted into the strobe lights, everything illuminated and thrown back into darkness, faces appearing and vanishing, appearing and vanishing, like flashbacks, like visions. Even the woman on crutches was trying to dance.

"Mika!" Elsie yelled.

She made it to the other side of the floor and stumbled out onto the deck. The door slammed tight behind her, the engine jackhammering the bones of her chest. She squinted at the stars, scattered Braille. She looked down toward the stern and then, finally, made out the shape of her sister's back.

Mika was smoking, a towel pulled tight around her, a stick of celery clutched in her other fist. In front of her, the moon cast a blurry drop cloth on the sea. "Maybe Pam would want this," she shouted over the waves, when Elsie joined her.

"It doesn't matter," Elsie shouted back. She draped the bathing suit around Mika's neck, and Mika moved her towel out of the way so Elsie could tie it. Music ricocheted off the water. Elsie adjusted the suit carefully, and then collected Mika's bleached, heavy hair in her hands and began to wring it out. Coil and wring. Coil and wring. The propeller's wash roiled into darkness. "I couldn't find you," she said. Her heart knocked around, all the pieces of it, dice in a cup.

"I'm here," Mika said.

ACKNOWLEDGMENTS

I am particularly grateful to my agent, Julie Barer, my editor, Caroline Zancan, and the wonderful team at Holt. Many thanks also to the MacDowell Colony, Yaddo, the St. Botolph Club Foundation, and the Elizabeth George Foundation for their support of this book.

ABOUT THE AUTHOR

Emma Duffy-Comparone is a graduate of the Boston University MFA program. Her fiction has appeared in *Ploughshares, New England Review, One Story, AGNI, The Sun,* the *Pushcart Prize XXXIX* and *XLI,* and elsewhere. She lives in Somerville, Massachusetts, and is an assistant professor of creative writing at Merrimack College.